IT

IT was a massive caricature of a man: a huge thing like an irregular mud doll, clumsily made. It quivered and parts of it glistened and parts of it were dried and crumbly. Half of the lower left part of its face was gone, giving it a lopsided look.

IT had no perceptible mouth or nose, and its eyes were crooked, one higher than the other, both a dingy brown with no whites at all.

IT had no mercy, no laughter, no beauty. It had strength and great intelligence . . . and . . . perhaps . . . it could not be destroyed!

"... Whether or not I ever really discovered Sturgeon's secret is a moot question. It is pretty hard to dissect laughing gas with a scalpel. Wit and spontaneity are far too evasive, they are brilliant gaseous material all too soon exploded and vanished!
—Ray Bradbury

Also by Theodore Sturgeon on the Ballantine
Books list:

MORE THAN HUMAN

available at your local bookstore

Not Without Sorcery

THEODORE STURGEON

BALLANTINE BOOKS • NEW YORK

To MARY MAIR
who in spite of the envy
of angels will live
forever.

Copyright 1939, 1940, 1941, 1946, 1947
by Street and Smith for
Astounding Science Fiction and *Unknown Worlds*
Copyright 1948 by Theodore Sturgeon

SBN 345-24664-0-150

First Printing: June, 1961
Second Printing: December, 1975

Printed in the United States of America

BALLANTINE BOOKS
A Division of Random House, Inc.
201 East 50th Street, New York, N.Y. 10022

Contents

Preface

That all the rules of story-telling be violated, let us begin by introducing a character who has nothing to do with anything else in this book.

His name is Gately, and he made a hole-in-one.

Gately is not a professional golfer. He had bought his first set of clubs five weeks and three days before the great event. He had risen that morning with no intention of playing golf. He had a toothache. He wanted to go to the office—he was in the marine canvas field, and was scheduled to attempt a large deal for the manufacture of Saudi Arabian flags—but realized that he would not be at his best with the toothache, and called his office. Then he called his dentist and made an appointment for eleven a.m. At nine-twenty-three, his dentist's wife stepped on a roller-skate left on the top of the stairs by her seven-year-old daughter. At nine-forty the dentist's secretary called Gately and cancelled the appointment. At that point Gately's tooth had ceased to trouble him; but since he had already secured a day's freedom from the office, he decided to take advantage of it to pursue his new hobby, bolf.

A caddy was assigned to Gately, and Gately had to wait four minutes for him while the caddy heard the rest of a pornographic anecdote being told him in the locker room by the pro.

Gately played the first four holes in a manner hardly worth recounting, except for his performance at the second, where he took eighteen strokes to get out of a water-hazard. At the fifth, he nudged his ball once on the positioning try, and his patent tee leaned over five degrees. On the backswing his right foot slipped a trifle

1

on the fore end of a large earthworm. He drove. The ball, badly sliced, bulleted into the rough, where it caromed off the concrete filling of the limb-socket of a gnarled oak. It began to cross the fairway, but was buoyed up by a sudden hearty breeze. Its course changed; it rolled to the green. It struck a grasshopper in midstride. The insect tried to take off but instead kicked the ball violently. The arrival point of the ball was thereby altered three sixty-fourths of an inch and it rolled to the cup, where after deliberation round the rim, it overbalanced and dropped in.

Now, should we consider one tenth of one percent of the factors involved in this hole-in-one, we would find:

That the dentist's daughter was arrested in the process of putting away her roller skates by the advent, on the radio, of one Uncle Gerard, who read the comics over the air, and who told his young listeners that tomorrow was their birthday, and if they looked behind the umbrella stand, they would find a present—*if* they had been good. And it happened to be the day before Gately's dentist's daughter's birthday.

That four days previous to the great event, a man called Markell had caught a bad cold. Mr. Markell was a free-lance airplane pilot, in the crop-dusting game, who had been hired by a farmer in Ohio to seed a thunder-cloud with dry ice to make some rain for the farmer's soybeans. Mr. Markell, when approaching the critical point in the thunderhead, had placed his hand on the release lever, and then had sneezed, sprinkling the cloud eight seconds early. Through a certain chain of meteorological events, this action had the ultimate result of generating the sudden brisk breeze which lofted Gately's caroming golfball.

That, four years before, the greens committee of Gately's golf club decided to leave the oak tree in the rough at the fifth, but to have a tree surgeon look at the dying limb on the north side. The surgeon had decided, for reasons of fee which were important because he was about to run off with the wife of his partner, to amputate the limb and fill the socket with a special concrete.

That, eight years before, Gately's dentist's wife had come to a decision in regard to increasing Gately's dentist's family.

That, sixty years previously, a squirrel, an extraordinarily simple-minded squirrel, had buried an acorn on the site of what was to be Gately's golf course.

That, twelve hundred and sixty-two years before, a wildcat sprained its right foreleg in pursuit of a squirrel, making it possible for the squirrel to transmit its excess stupidity along with its survival characteristics to its descendants, one of which planted the oak.

That, two thousand years ago, a bibulous and inventive mariner generated the first version of the anecdote with which the pro delayed Mr. Gately's caddy, thus timing Mr. Gately's slice on the fifth with Mr. Gately's earthworm, small breeze, and grasshopper.

There is obviously no point in going on into the permutations involved, for example, in the order for Saudi Arabian flags, nor in the psychic trauma which led Mr. Gately to add something to his social position by joining the golf club. There is a point in having come so far with it; namely, that Gately's hole-in-one was, in truth, a far more remarkable thing than it appeared. For had any one of the above factors been altered, he would not have accomplished the feat. And there are many, many more factors.

We have been regarding a hole-in-one in this light because it is remarkable enough in itself to lead us to wonder at its causes. But many an unremarkable thing has an interesting background. Mr. Gately's hole-in-one violates the laws of probability to a shocking extent. So, by the same token, does the fact that the marks on this page form the particular words they do, that That Man ever got into the White House, or even that our reader is alive at all. The odds are incalculably against such things. When the loss of the lid of an ash-can in Milwaukee can be traced to the jest of a Caesar, and when the romantic hesitancies of a prehistoric Eohippus show up in the fourth race at Pimlico, then the reader is counseled to think more than twice before he brands anything in this volume as "improbable."

New York,
January, 1948

I have been asked repeatedly how this story was written, or how one gets ideas like this, or what one has to be or go through to be able to write such a horror.

I can only answer that it wrote itself. It unfolded without any signal effort on my part from the first sentence. The names of the characters were taken off my ubiquitous coffee-maker. I was supremely happy as I wrote it—no twistings, no warpings, no depression. Possibly it was catharsis—in other words, I was feeling so good that I took what poisons were in me at the moment and got rid of them in one pure plash of putrescence. It was very easy to do and I wish I could do it again.

It

It walked in the woods.

It was never born. It existed. Under the pine needles the fires burn, deep and smokeless in the mold. In heat and in darkness and decay there is growth. There is life and there is growth. It grew, but it was not alive. It walked unbreathing through the woods, and thought and saw and was hideous and strong, and it was not born and it did not live. It grew and moved about without living.

It crawled out of the darkness and hot damp mold into the cool of a morning. It was huge. It was lumped and crusted with its own hateful substances, and pieces of it dropped off as it went its way, dropped off and lay writhing, and stilled, and sank putrescent into the forest loam.

It had no mercy, no laughter, no beauty. It had strength and great intelligence. And—perhaps it could not be destroyed. It crawled out of its mound in the wood and lay pulsing in the sunlight for a long moment. Patches of it shone wetly in the golden glow, parts of it were nubbled and flaked. And whose dead bones had given it the form of a man?

It scrabbled painfully with its half-formed hands, beating the ground and the bole of a tree. It rolled and lifted itself up on its crumbling elbows, and it tore up a great handful of herbs and shredded them against its chest, and it paused and gazed at the gray-green juices with intelligent calm. It wavered to its feet, and seized a young sapling and destroyed it, folding the slender trunk back on itself again and again, watching attentively the useless, fibered splinters. And it snatched up a fear-frozen field-creature, crushing it slowly, letting blood and pulpy flesh and fur ooze from between its fingers, run down and rot on the forearms.

It began searching.

Kimbo drifted through the tall grasses like a puff of dust, his bushy tail curled tightly over his back and his long jaws agape. He ran with an easy lope, loving his freedom and the power of his flanks and furry shoulders. His tongue lolled listlessly over his lips. His lips were black and serrated, and each tiny pointed liplet swayed with his doggy gallop. Kimbo was all dog, all healthy animal.

He leaped high over a boulder and landed with a startled yelp as a longeared cony shot from its hiding place under the rock. Kimbo hurtled after it, grunting with each great thrust of his legs. The rabbit bounced just ahead of him, keeping its distance, its ears flattened on its curving back and its little legs nibbling away at distance hungrily. It stopped, and Kimbo pounced, and the rabbit shot away at a tangent and popped into a hollow log. Kimbo yelped again and rushed snuffling at the log, and knowing his failure, curvetted but once around the stump and ran on into the forest. The thing that watched from the wood raised its crusted arms and waited for Kimbo.

Kimbo sensed it there, standing dead-still by the

path. To him it was a bulk which smelled of carrion not fit to roll in, and he snuffled distastefully and ran to pass it.

The thing let him come abreast and dropped a heavy twisted fist on him. Kimbo saw it coming and curled up tight as he ran, and the hand clipped stunningly on his rump, sending him rolling and yipping down the slope. Kimbo straddled to his feet, shook his head, shook his body with a deep growl, came back to the silent thing with green murder in his eyes. He walked stiffly, straight-legged, his tail as low as his lowered head and a ruff of fury round his neck. The thing raised its arms again, waited.

Kimbo slowed, then flipped himself through the air at the monster's throat. His jaws closed on it; his teeth clicked together through a mass of filth, and he fell choking and snarling at its feet. The thing leaned down and struck twice, and after the dog's back was broken, it sat beside him and began to tear him apart.

"Be back in an hour or so," said Alton Drew, picking up his rifle from the corner behind the wood box. His brother laughed.

"Old Kimbo 'bout runs your life, Alton," he said.

"Ah, I know the ol' devil," said Alton. "When I whistle for him for half an hour and he don't show up, he's in a jam or he's treed something wuth shootin' at. The ol' son of a gun calls me by not answerin'."

Cory Drew shoved a full glass of milk over to his nine-year-old daughter and smiled. "You think as much o' that houn' dog o' yours as I do of Babe here."

Babe slid off her chair and ran to her uncle. "Gonna catch me the bad fella, Uncle Alton?" she shrilled. The "bad fella" was Cory's invention—the one who lurked in corners ready to pounce on little girls who chased the chickens and played around mowing machines and hurled green apples with a powerful young arm at the sides of the hogs, to hear the synchronized thud and grunt; little girls who swore with an Austrian accent like an ex-hired man they had had; who dug caves in haystacks till they tipped over, and kept pet crawfish in tomorrow's milk cans, and rode work horses to a lather in the night pasture.

"Get back here and keep away from Uncle Alton's gun!" said Cory. "If you see the bad fella, Alton, chase him back here. He has a date with Babe here for that stunt of hers last night." The preceding evening, Babe had kind-heartedly poured pepper on the cows' salt block.

"Don't worry, kiddo," grinned her uncle, "I'll bring you the bad fella's hide if he don't get me first."

Alton Drew walked up the path toward the wood, thinking about Babe. She was a phenomenon—a pampered farm child. Ah well—she had to be. They'd both loved Clissa Drew, and she'd married Cory, and they had to love Clissa's child. Funny thing, love. Alton was a man's man, and thought things out that way; and his reaction to love was a strong and frightened one. He knew what love was because he felt it still for his brother's wife and would feel it as long as he lived for Babe. It led him through his life, and yet he embarrassed himself by thinking of it. Loving a dog was an easy thing, because you and the old devil could love one another completely without talking about it. The smell of gun smoke and wet fur in the rain were perfume enough for Alton Drew, a grunt of satisfaction and the scream of something hunted and hit were poetry enough. They weren't like love for a human, that choked his throat so he could not say words he could not have thought of anyway. So Alton loved his dog Kimbo and his Winchester for all to see, and let his love for his brother's women, Clissa and Babe, eat at him quietly and unmentioned.

His quick eyes saw the fresh indentations in the soft earth behind the boulder, which showed where Kimbo had turned and leaped with a single surge, chasing the rabbit. Ignoring the tracks, he looked for the nearest place where a rabbit might hide, and strolled over to the stump. Kimbo had been there, he saw, and had been there too late. "You're an ol' fool," muttered Alton. "Y' can't catch a cony by chasin' it. You want to cross him up some way." He gave a peculiar trilling whistle, sure that Kimbo was digging frantically under some nearby stump for a rabbit that was three counties away by now. No answer. A little puzzled, Alton went back to the path. "He never done this before," he said softly.

He cocked his .32-40 and cradled it. At the county fair someone had once said of Alton Drew that he could shoot at a handful of corn and peas thrown in the air and hit only the corn. Once he split a bullet on the blade of a knife and put two candles out. He had no need to fear anything that could be shot at. That's what he believed.

The thing in the woods looked curiously down at what it had done to Kimbo, and tried to moan the way Kimbo had before he died. It stood a minute storing away facts in its foul, unemotional mind. Blood was warm. The sunlight was warm. Things that moved and bore fur had a muscle to force the thick liquid through tiny tubes in their bodies. The liquid coagulated after a time. The liquid on rooted green things was thinner and the loss of a limb did not mean loss of life. It was very interesting, but the thing, the mold with a mind, was not pleased. Neither was it displeased. Its accidental urge was a thirst for knowledge, and it was only—interested.

It was growing late, and the sun reddened and rested awhile on the hilly horizon, teaching the clouds to be inverted flames. The thing threw up its head suddenly, noticing the dusk. Night was ever a strange thing, even for those of us who have known it in life. It would have been frightening for the monster had it been capable of fright, but it could only be curious; it could only reason from what it had observed.

What was happening? It was getting harder to see. Why? It threw its shapeless head from side to side. It was true—things were dim, and growing dimmer.

Things were changing shape, taking on a new and darker color. What did the creatures it had crushed and torn apart see? How did they see? The larger one, the one that had attacked, had used two organs in its head. That must have been it, because after the thing had torn off two of the dog's legs it had struck at the hairy muzzle; and the dog, seeing the blow coming, had dropped folds of skin over the organs—closed its eyes. Ergo, the dog saw with its eyes. But then after the dog was dead, and its body still, repeated blows had had no effect on the eyes. They remained open and staring. The logical conclusion was, then, that a being that had ceased to live and breathe and move about lost the use of its eyes. It must be that to lose sight was, conversely, to die. Dead things did not walk about. They lay down and did not move. Therefore the thing in the wood concluded that it must be dead, and so it lay down by the path, not far away from Kimbo's scattered body, lay down and believed itself dead.

Alton Drew came up through the dusk to the wood. He was frankly worried. He whistled again, and then called, and there was still no response, and he said again, "The ol' flea-bus never done this before," and shook his heavy head. It was past milking time, and Cory would need him. "Kimbo!" he roared. The cry echoed through the shadows, and Alton flipped on the safety catch of his rifle and put the butt on the ground beside the path. Leaning on it, he took off his cap and scratched the back of his head, wondering. The rifle butt sank into what he thought was soft earth; he staggered and stepped into the chest of the thing that lay beside the path. His foot went up to the ankle in its yielding rottenness, and he swore and jumped back.

"Whew! Somp'n sure dead as hell there! Ugh!" He swabbed at his boot with a handful of leaves while the monster lay in the growing blackness with the edges of the deep footprint in its chest sliding into it, filling it up. It lay there regarding him dimly out of its muddy eyes, thinking it was dead because of the darkness, watching the articulation of Alton Drew's joints, wondering at this new uncautious creature.

Alton cleaned the butt of his gun with more leaves and went on up the path, whistling anxiously for Kimbo.

Clissa Drew stood in the door of the milk shed, very lovely in red-checked gingham and a blue apron. Her hair was clean yellow, parted in the middle and stretched tautly back to a heavy braided knot. "Cory! Alton!" she called a little sharply.

"Well?" Cory responded gruffly from the barn, where he was stripping off the Ayrshire. The dwindling streams of milk plopped pleasantly into the froth of a full pail.

"I've called and called," said Clissa. "Supper's cold, and Babe won't eat until you come. Why—where's Alton?"

Cory grunted, heaved the stool out of the way, threw over the stanchion lock and slapped the Ayrshire on the rump. The cow backed and filled like a towboat, clattered down the line and out into the barn-yard. "Ain't back yet."

"Not back?" Clissa came in and stood beside him as he sat by the next cow, put his forehead against the warm flank. "But, Cory, he said he'd—"

"Yeh, yeh, I know. He said he'd be back fer the milkin'. I heard him. Well, he ain't."

"And you have to— Oh, Cory, I'll help you finish up. Alton would be back if he could. Maybe he's—"

"Maybe he's treed a blue jay," snapped her husband. "Him an' that damn dog." He gestured hugely with one hand while the other went on milking. "I got twenty-six head o' cows to milk. I got pigs to feed an' chickens to put to bed. I got to toss hay for the mare and turn the team out. I got harness to mend and a wire down in the night pasture. I got wood to split an' carry." He milked for a moment in silence, chewing on his lip. Clissa stood twisting her hands together, trying to think of something to stem the tide. It wasn't the first time Alton's hunting had interfered with the chores. "So I got to go ahead with it. I can't interfere with Alton's spoorin.' Every damn time that hound o' his smells out a squirrel I go without my supper. I'm gettin' sick and—"

"Oh, I'll help you!" said Clissa. She was thinking of the spring, when Kimbo had held four hundred pounds of raging black bear at bay until Alton could put a bullet in its brain, the time Babe had found a bearcub and started to carry it home, and had fallen into a freshet, cutting her head. You can't hate a dog that has saved your child for you, she thought.

"You'll do nothin' of the kind!" Cory growled. "Get back to the house. You'll find work enough there. I'll be along when I can. Dammit, Clissa, don't cry! I didn't mean to—Oh, shucks!" He got up and put his arms around her. "I'm wrought up," he said. "Go on now. I'd no call to speak that way to you. I'm sorry. Go back to Babe. I'll put a stop to this for good tonight. I've had enough. There's work here for four farmers an' all we've got is me an' that ... that huntsman.

"Go on now, Clissa."

"All right," she said into his shoulder. "But, Cory, hear him out first when he comes back. He might be unable to come back. He might be unable to come back this time. Maybe he ... he—"

"Ain't nothin' kin hurt my brother that a bullet will hit. He can take care of himself. He's got no excuse good enough this time. Go on, now. Make the kid eat."

Clissa went back to the house, her young face furrowed. If Cory quarreled with Alton now and drove him away, what with the drought and the creamery about to close and all, they just couldn't manage. Hiring a man was out of the question. Cory'd have to work himself to death, and he just wouldn't be able to make it. No one man could. She sighed and went into the house. It was seven o'clock, and the milking not done yet. Oh, why did Alton have to—

Babe was in bed at nine when Clissa heard Cory in

the shed, slinging the wire cutters into a corner. "Alton back yet?" they both said at once as Cory stepped into the kitchen; and as she shook her head he clumped over to the stove, and lifting a lid, spat into the coals. "Come to bed," he said.

She laid down her stitching and looked at his broad back. He was twenty-eight, and he walked and acted like a man ten years older, and looked like a man five years younger. "I'll be up in a while," Clissa said.

Cory glanced at the corner behind the wood box where Alton's rifle usually stood, then made an unspellable, disgusted sound and sat down to take off his heavy muddy shoes.

"It's after nine," Clissa volunteered timidly. Cory said nothing, reaching for house slippers.

"Cory, you're not going to—"

"Not going to what?"

"Oh, nothing. I just thought that maybe Alton—"

"Alton," Cory flared. "The dog goes hunting field mice. Alton goes hunting the dog. Now you want me to go hunting Alton. That's what you want?"

"I just—He was never this late before."

"I won't do it! Go out lookin' for him at nine o'clock in the night? I'll be damned! He has no call to use us so, Clissa."

Clissa said nothing. She went to the stove, peered into the wash boiler, set aside at the back of the range. When she turned around, Cory had his shoes and coat on again.

"I knew you'd go," she said. Her voice smiled though she did not.

"I'll be back durned soon," said Cory. "I don't reckon he's strayed far. It is late. I ain't feared for him, but—" He broke his 12-gauge shotgun, looked through the barrels, slipped two shells in the breech and a box of them into his pocket. "Don't wait up," he said over his shoulder as he went out.

"I won't," Clissa replied to the closed door, and went back to her stitching by the lamp.

The path up the slope to the wood was very dark

when Cory went up it, peering and calling. The air was chill and quiet, and a fetid odor of mold hung in it. Cory blew the taste of it out through impatient nostrils, drew it in again with the next breath, and swore. "Nonsense," he muttered. "Houn' dawg. Huntin', at ten in th' night, too. Alton!" he bellowed. "Alton Drew!" Echoes answered him, and he entered the wood. The huddled thing he passed in the dark heard him and felt the vibrations of his foot-steps and did not move because it thought it was dead.

Cory strode on, looking around and ahead and not down since his feet knew the path.

"Alton!"

"That you, Cory?"

Cory Drew froze. That corner of the wood was thickly set and as dark as a burial vault. The voice he heard was choked, quiet, penetrating.

"Alton?"

"I found Kimbo, Cory."

"Where the hell have you been?" shouted Cory furiously. He disliked this pitch-darkness; he was afraid at the tense hopelessness of Alton's voice, and he mistrusted his ability to stay angry at his brother.

"I called him, Cory. I whistled at him, an' the ol' devil didn't answer."

"I can say the same for you, you . . . you louse. Why weren't you to milkin'? Where are you? You caught in a trap?"

"The houn' never missed answerin' me before, you know," said the tight, monotonous voice from the darkness.

"Alton! What the devil's the matter with you? What do I care if your mutt didn't answer? Where——"

"I guess because he ain't never died before," said Alton, refusing to be interrupted.

"You *what*?" Cory clicked his lips together twice and then said, "Alton, you turned crazy? What's that you say?"

"Kimbo's dead."

"Kim . . . oh! Oh!" Cory was seeing that picture

again in his mind— Babe sprawled unconscious in the freshet, and Kimbo raging and snapping against a monster bear, holding her back until Alton could get there. "What happened, Alton?" he asked more quietly.

"I aim to find out. Someone tore him up."

"Tore him up?"

"There ain't a bit of him left tacked together, Cory. Every damn joint in his body tore apart. Guts out of him."

"Good God! Bear, you reckon?"

"No bear, nor nothin' on four legs. He's all here. None of him's been et. Whoever done it just killed him an'—tore him up."

"Good God!" Cory said again. "Who could've—" There was a long silence, then. "Come 'long home," he said almost gently. "There's no call for you to set up by him all night."

"I'll set. I aim to be here at sunup, an' I'm going to start trackin', an' I'm goin' to keep trackin' till I find the one done this job on Kimbo."

"You're drunk or crazy, Alton."

"I ain't drunk. You can think what you like about the rest of it. I'm stickin' here."

"We got a farm back yonder. Remember? I ain't going to milk twenty-six head o' cows again in the mornin' like I did jest now, Alton."

"Somebody's got to. I can't be there. I guess you'll just have to, Cory."

"You dirty scum!" Cory screamed. "You'll come back with me now or I'll know why!"

Alton's voice was still tight, half-sleepy. "Don't you come no nearer, bud."

Cory kept moving toward Alton's voice.

"I said"—the voice was very quiet now—*"stop where you are."* Cory kept coming. A sharp click told of the release of the .32-40's safety. Cory stopped.

"You got your gun on me, Alton?" Cory whispered.

"Thass right, bud. You ain't a-trompin' up these tracks for me. I need 'em at sunup."

A full minute passed, and the only sound in the blackness was that of Cory's pained breathing. Finally:

"I got my gun, too, Alton. Come home."

"You can't see to shoot me."

"We're even on that."

"We ain't. I know just where you stand, Cory. I been here four hours."

"My gun scatters."

"My gun kills."

Without another word Cory Drew turned on his heel and stamped back to the farm.

Black and liquidescent it lay in the blackness, not alive, not understanding death, believing itself dead. Things that were alive saw and moved about. Things that were not alive could do neither. It rested its muddy gaze on the line of trees at the crest of the rise, and deep within it thoughts trickled wetly. It lay huddled, dividing its newfound facts, dissecting them as it had dissected live things when there was light, comparing, concluding, pigeonholing.

The trees at the top of the slope could just be seen, as their trunks were a fraction of a shade lighter than the dark sky behind them. At length they, too, disappeared, and for a moment sky and trees were a monotone. The thing knew it was dead now, and like many a being before it, it wondered how long it must stay like this. And then the sky beyond the trees grew a little lighter. That was a manifestly impossible occurrence, thought the thing, but it could see it and it must be so. Did dead things live again? That was curious. What about dismembered dead things? It would wait and see.

The sun came hand over hand up a beam of light. A bird somewhere made a high yawning peep, and as an owl killed a shrew, a skunk pounced on another, so that the night shift deaths and those of the day could go on without cessation. Two flowers nodded archly to each other, comparing their pretty clothes. A dragon fly nymph decided it was tired of looking serious and cracked its back open, to crawl out and dry gauzily.

The first golden ray sheared down between the trees, through the grasses, passed over the mass in the shadowed bushes. "I am alive again," thought the thing that could not possibly live. "I am alive, for I see clearly." It stood up on its thick legs, up into the golden glow. In a little while the wet flakes that had grown during the night dried in the sun, and when it took its first steps, they cracked off and a small shower of them fell away. It walked up the slope to find Kimbo, to see if he, too, were alive again.

Babe let the sun come into her room by opening her eyes. Uncle Alton was gone—that was the first thing that ran through her head. Dad had come home last night and had shouted at mother for an hour. Alton was plumb crazy. He'd turned a gun on his own brother. If Alton ever came ten feet into Cory's land, Cory would fill him so full of holes, he'd look like a tumbleweed. Alton was lazy, shiftless, selfish, and one or two other things of questionable taste but undoubted vividness. Babe knew her father. Uncle Alton would never be safe in this county.

She bounced out of bed in the enviable way of the very young, and ran to the window. Cory was trudging down to the night pasture with two bridles over his arm, to get the team. There were kitchen noises from downstairs.

Babe ducked her head in the washbowl and shook off the water like a terrier before she toweled. Trailing clean shirt and dungarees, she went to the head of the stairs, slid into the shirt, and began her morning ritual with the trousers. One step down was a step through the right leg. One more, and she was into the left. Then, bouncing step by step on both feet, buttoning one button per step, she reached the bottom fully dressed and ran into the kitchen.

"Didn't Uncle Alton come back a-tall, Mum?"

"Morning, Babe. No, dear." Clissa was too quiet, smiling too much, Babe thought shrewdly. Wasn't happy.

"Where'd he go, Mum?"

"We don't know, Babe. Sit down and eat your breakfast."

"What's a misbegotten, Mum?" Babe asked suddenly. Her mother nearly dropped the dish she was drying. "Babe! You must never say that again!"

"Oh. Well, why is Uncle Alton, then?"

"Why is he what?"

Babe's mouth muscled around an outsize spoonful of oatmeal. "A misbe——"

"Babe!"

"All right, Mum," said Babe with her mouth full. "Well, why?"

"I told Cory not to shout last night," Clissa said half to herself.

"Well, whatever it means, he isn't," said Babe with finality. "Did he go hunting again?"

"He went to look for Kimbo, darling."

"Kimbo? Oh Mummy, is Kimbo gone, too? Didn't he come back either?"

"No dear. Oh, please, Babe, stop asking questions!"

"All right. Where do you think they went?"

"Into the north woods. Be quiet."

Babe gulped away at her breakfast. An idea struck her; and as she thought of it she ate slower and slower, and cast more and more glances at her mother from under the lashes of her tilted eyes. It would be awful if daddy did anything to Uncle Alton. Someone ought to warn him.

Babe was halfway to the woods when Alton's .32-40 sent echoes giggling up and down the valley.

Cory was in the south thirty, riding a cultivator and cussing at the team of grays when he heard the gun. "Hoa," he called to the horses, and sat a moment to listen to the sound. "One-two-three. Four," he counted. "Saw someone, blasted away at him. Had a chance to take aim and give him another, careful. My God!" He threw up the cultivator points and steered the team into the shade of three oaks. He hobbled the gelding with swift tosses of a spare strap, and headed for the woods. "Alton a killer," he murmered, and doubled back to the house for his gun. Clissa was standing just outside the door.

"Get shells!" he snapped and flung into the house. Clissa followed him. He was strapping his hunting knife on before she could get a box off the shelf. "Cory—"

"Hear that gun, did you? Alton's off his nut. He don't waste lead. He shot at someone just then, and he wasn't fixin' to shoot pa'tridges when I saw him last. He was out to get a man. Gimme my gun."

"Cory, Babe—"

"You keep her here. Oh, God, this is a helluva mess. I can't stand much more." Cory ran out the door.

Clissa caught his arm: "Cory I'm trying to tell you. Babe isn't here. I've called, and she isn't here."

Cory's heavy, young-old face tautened. "Babe— Where did you last see her?"

"Breakfast." Clissa was crying now.

"She say where she was going?"

"No. She asked a lot of questions about Alton and where he'd gone."

"Did you say?"

Clissa's eyes widened, and she nodded, biting the back of her hand.

"You shouldn't ha' done that, Clissa," he gritted, and ran toward the woods, Clissa looking after him, and in that moment she could have killed herself.

Cory ran with his head up, straining with his legs and lungs and eyes at the long path. He puffed up the slope to the woods, agonized for breath after the forty-five minutes' heavy going. He couldn't even notice the damp smell of mold in the air.

He caught a movement in a thicket to his right, and dropped. Struggling to keep his breath, he crept forward until he could see clearly. There was something in there, all right. Something black, keeping still. Cory relaxed his legs and torso completely to make it easier for his heart to pump some strength back into them, and slowly raised the 12-gauge until it bore on the thing hidden in the thicket.

"Come out!" Cory said when he could speak.

Nothing happened.

"Come out or by God I'll shoot!" rasped Cory.

There was a long moment of silence, and his finger tightened on the trigger.

"You asked for it," he said, and as he fired, the thing leaped sideways into the open, screaming.

It was a thin little man dressed in sepulchral black, and bearing the rosiest baby-face Cory had ever seen. The face was twisted with fright and pain. The man scrambled to his feet and hopped up and down saying over and over, "Oh, my hand. Don't shoot again! Oh, my hand. Don't shoot again!" He stopped after a bit, when Cory had climbed to his feet, and he regarded the farmer out of sad china-blue eyes. "You shot me," he said reproachfully, holding up a little bloody hand. "Oh, my goodness."

Cory said, "Now, who the hell are you?"

The man immediately became hysterical, mouthing such a flood of broken sentences that Cory stepped back a pace and half-raised his gun in self-defense. It seemed to consist mostly of "I lost my papers," and "I didn't do it," and "It was horrible. Horrible. Horrible," and "The dead man," and "Oh, don't shoot again."

Cory tried twice to ask him a question, and then he stepped over and knocked the man down. He lay on the ground writhing and moaning and blubbering and putting his bloody hand to his mouth where Cory had hit him.

"Now what's going on around here?"

The man rolled over and sat up. "I didn't do it!" he sobbed. "I didn't. I was walking along and I heard the gun and I heard some swearing and an awful scream and I went over there and peeped and I saw the dead

man and I ran away and you came and I hid and you
shot me and—"

"*Shut up!*" The man did, as if a switch has been
thrown. "Now," said Cory, pointing along the path,
"you say there's a dead man up there?"

The man nodded and began crying in earnest. Cory
helped him up. "Follow this path back to my farm-
house," he said. "Tell my wife to fix up your hand.
Don't tell her anything else. And wait there until I
come. Hear?"

"Yes. Thank you. Oh, thank you. *Snff.*"

"Go on now." Cory gave him a gentle shove in the
right direction and went alone, in cold fear, up the path
to the spot where he had found Alton the night before.

He found him here now, too, and Kimbo. Kimbo
and Alton had spent several years together in the
deepest friendship; they had hunted and fought and
slept together, and the lives they owed each other were
finished now. They were dead together.

It was terrible that they died the same way. Cory
Drew was a strong man, but he gasped and fainted
dead away when he saw what the thing of the mold
had done to his brother and his brother's dog.

The little man in black hurried down the path,
whimpering and holding his injured hand as if he
rather wished he could limp with it. After a while the
whimper faded away, and the hurried stride changed to
a walk as the gibbering terror of the last hour receded.
He drew two deep breaths, said: "My goodness!" and
felt almost normal. He bound a linen handkerchief
around his wrist, but the hand kept bleeding. He tried
the elbow, and that made it hurt. So he stuffed the
handkerchief back in his pocket and simply waved the
hand stupidly in the air until the blood clotted. He did
not see the great moist horror that clumped along behind him, although his nostrils crinkled with its foulness.

The monster had three holes close together on its
chest, and one hole in the middle of its slimy forehead.

It had three close-set pits in its back and one on the back of its head. These marks were where Alton Drew's bullets had struck and passed through. Half of the monster's shapeless face was sloughed away, and there was a deep indentation on its shoulder. This was what Alton Drew's gun butt had done after he clubbed it and struck at the thing that would not lie down after he put his four bullets through it. When these things happened the monster was not hurt or angry. It only wondered why Alton Drew acted that way. Now it followed the little man without hurrying at all, match-his stride step by step and dropping little particles of muck behind it.

The little man went on out of the wood and stood with his back against a big tree at the forest's edge, and he thought. Enough had happened to him here. What good would it do to stay and face a horrible murder inquest, just to continue this silly, vague search? There was supposed to be the ruin of an old, old hunting lodge deep in this wood somewhere, and perhaps it would hold the evidence he wanted. But it was a vague report—vague enough to be forgotten without regret. It would be the height of foolishness to stay for all the hick-town red tape that would follow that ghastly affair back in the wood. Ergo, it would be ridiculous to follow that farmer's advice, to go to his house and wait for him. He would go back to town.

The monster was leaning against the other side of the big tree.

The little man snuffled disgustedly at a sudden overpowering odor of rot. He reached for his handkerchief, fumbled and dropped it. As he bent to pick it up, the monster's arm *whuffed* heavily in the air where his head had been—a blow that would certainly have removed that baby-face protuberance. The man stood up and would have put the handkerchief to his nose had it not been so bloody. The creature behind the tree lifted its arm again just as the little man tossed the handkerchief 'away and stepped out into the field, heading across country to the distant highway that would take him back to town. The monster pounced on the handkerchief, picked it up, studied it, tore it across several times and inspected the tattered edges. Then it gazed vacantly at the disappearing figure of the little man, and finding him no longer interesting, turned back into the woods.

Babe broke into a trot at the sound of the shots. It was important to warn Uncle Alton about what her father had said, but it was more interesting to find out what he had bagged. Oh, he'd bagged it, all right. Uncle Alton never fired without killing. This was about the first time she had ever heard him blast away like that. Must be a bear, she thought excitedly, tripping over a root, sprawling, rolling to her feet again, without noticing the tumble. She'd love to have another bearskin in her room. Where would she put it? Maybe they could line it and she could have it for a blanket. Uncle Alton could sit on it and read to her in the evening— Oh, no. No. Not with this trouble between him and dad. Oh, if she could only do something! She tried to run faster, worried and anticipating, but she was out of breath and went more slowly instead.

At the top of the rise by the edge of the woods she stopped and looked back. Far down in the valley lay the south thirty. She scanned it carefully, looking for her father. The new furrows and the old were sharply defined, and her keen eyes saw immediately that Cory had left the line with the cultivator and had angled the team over to the shade trees without finishing his row. That wasn't like him. She could see the team now, and Cory's pale-blue denim was nowhere in sight. She giggled lightly to herself as she thought of the way she would fool her father. And the little sound of laughter drowned out, for her, the sound of Alton's hoarse dying scream.

She reached and crossed the path and slid through the brush beside it. The shots came from up around here somewhere. She stopped and listened several times, and then suddenly heard something coming toward her, fast. She ducked under cover, terrified, and a little baby-faced man in black, his blue eyes wide with horror, crashed blindly past her, the leather case he carried catching on the branches. It spun a moment and then fell right in front of her. The man never missed it.

Babe lay there for a long moment and then picked up the case and faded into the woods. Things were happening too fast for her. She wanted Uncle Alton, but she dared not call. She stopped again and strained her ears. Back toward the edge of the wood she heard her father's voice, and another's—probably the man who had dropped the brief case. She dared not go over there. Filled with enjoyable terror, she thought hard, then snapped her fingers in triumph. She and Alton had played Injun many times up here; they had a whole repertoire of secret signals. She had practiced birdcalls until she knew them better than the birds themselves. What would it be? Ah—blue jay. She threw back her head and by some youthful alchemy produced a nerve-shattering screech that would have done justice to any jay that ever flew. She repeated it, and then twice more.

The response was immediate—the call of a blue jay, four times, spaced two and two. Babe nodded to herself happily. That was the signal that they were to meet immediately at The Place. The Place was a hide-out that he had discovered and shared with her, and not another soul knew of it; an angle of rock beside a stream not far away. It wasn't exactly a cave, but almost. Enough so to be entrancing. Babe trotted happily away toward the brook. She had just known that Uncle Alton would remember the call of the blue jay, and what it meant.

In the tree that arched over Alton's scattered body perched a large jay bird, preening itself and shining in the sun. Quite unconscious of the presence of death, hardly noticing the Babe's realistic cry, it screamed again four times, two and two.

It took Cory more than a moment to recover himself from what he had seen. He turned away from it and leaned weakly against a pine, panting. Alton. That was Alton lying there, in—parts.

"God! God, God, God—"

Gradually his strength returned, and he forced himself to turn again. Stepping carefully, he bent and picked up the .32-40. Its barrel was bright and clean, but the butt and stock were smeared with some kind of stinking rottenness. Where had he seen the stuff before? Somewhere—no matter. He cleaned it off absently, throwing the befouled bandanna away afterward. Through his mind ran Alton's words—was that only last night?— *"I'm goin' start trackin'. An' I'm goin' to keep trackin' till I find the one done this job on Kimbo."*

Cory searched shrinkingly until he found Alton's box of shells. The box was wet and sticky. That made it—better, somehow. A bullet wet with Alton's blood was the right thing to use. He went away a short distance, circled around till he found heavy footprints, then came back.

"I'm a-trackin' for you, bud," he whispered thickly, and began. Through the brush he followed its wavering spoor, amazed at the amount of filthy mold about, gradually associating it with the thing that had killed his brother. There was nothing in the world for him anymore but hate and doggedness. Cursing himself for not getting Alton home last night, he followed the tracks to the edge of the woods. They led him to a big tree there, and there he saw something else—the footprints of the little city man. Nearby lay some tattered scraps of linen, and—what was that?

Another set of prints—small ones. Small, stub-toed ones.

"Babe!"

No answer. The wind sighed. Somewhere a blue jay called.

Babe stopped and turned when she heard her father's voice, faint with distance, piercing.

"Listen at him holler," she crooned delightedly. "Gee, he sounds mad." She sent a jay bird's call disrespectfully back to him and hurried to The Place.

It consisted of a mammoth boulder beside the brook. Some upheaval in the glacial age had cleft it, cutting out a huge V-shaped chunk. The widest part of the cleft was at the water's edge, and the narrowest was hidden by bushes. It made a little ceilingless room, rough and uneven and full of pot-holes and cavelets inside, and yet with quite a level floor. The open end was at the water's edge.

Babe parted the bushes and peered down the cleft.

"Uncle Alton!" she called softly. There was no answer. Oh, well, he'd be along. She scrambled in and slid down to the floor.

She loved it here. It was shaded and cool, and the chattering stream filled it with shifting golden lights and laughing gurgles. She called again, on principle, and then perched on an outcropping to wait. It was only then she realized that she still carried the little man's brief case.

She turned it over a couple of times and then opened it. It was divided in the middle by a leather wall. On one side were a few papers in a large yellow envelope, and on the other some sandwiches, a candy bar, and an apple. With a youngster's complacent acceptance of manna from heaven, Babe fell to. She saved one sandwich for Alton, mainly because she didn't like its highly spiced bologna. The rest made quite a feast.

She was a little worried when Alton hadn't arrived, even after she had consumed the apple core. She got up and tried to skim some flat pebbles across the roiling brook, and she stood on her hands, and she tried to think of a story to tell herself, and she tried just waiting. Finally, in desperation, she turned again to the brief case, took out the papers, curled up by the rocky wall and began to read them. It was something to do, anyway.

There was an old newspaper clipping that told about strange wills that people had left. An old lady had once left a lot of money to whoever would make the trip from the Earth to the Moon and back. Another had financed a home for cats whose masters and mistresses had died. A man left thousands of dollars to the first person who could solve a certain mathematical problem and prove his solution. But one item was blue-penciled. It was:

One of the strangest of wills still in force is that of Thaddeus M. Kirk, who died in 1920. It appears that he built an elaborate mausoleum with burial vaults for all the remains of his family. He collected and removed caskets from all over the country to fill the designated niches. Kirk was the last of his line; there were no relatives when he died. His will stated that the mausoleum was to be kept in repair permanently, and that a certain sum set aside as a reward for whoever could produce the body of his grandfather, Roger Kirk, whose niche is still empty. Anyone finding this body is eligible to receive a substantial fortune.

Babe yawned vaguely over this, but kept on reading because there was nothing else to do. Next was a thick sheet of business correspondence, bearing the letterhead of a firm of lawyers. The body of it ran:

In regard to your query regarding the will of Thaddeus Kirk, we are authorized to state that his grandfather was a man about five feet, five inches, whose left arm had been broken and who had a triangular silver plate set into his skull. There is no information as to the whereabouts of his death. He disappeared and was declared legally dead after the lapse of fourteen years.

The amount of the reward as stated in the will, plus accrued interest, now amounts to a fraction over sixty-two thousand dollars. This will be paid to anyone who produces the remains, providing that said remains answer descriptions kept in our private files.

There was more, but Babe was bored. She went on to the little black notebook. There was nothing in it but penciled and highly abbreviated records of visits to libraries; quotations from books with titles like "History of Angelina and Tyler Counties" and "Kirk Family History." Babe threw that aside, too. Where could Uncle Alton be?

She began to sing tunelessly, "Tumalumalum tum, ta ta ta," pretending to dance a minuet with flowing skirts like a girl she had seen in the movies. A rustle of the bushes at the entrance to The Place stopped her. She peeped upward, saw them being thrust aside. Quickly she ran to a tiny cul-de-sac in the rock wall, just big enough for her to hide in. She giggled at the thought of how surprised Uncle Alton would be when she jumped out at him.

She heard the newcomer come shuffling down the steep slope of the crevice and land heavily on the floor. There was something about the sound—What was it? It occurred to her that though it was a hard job for a big man like Uncle Alton to get through the little opening in the bushes, she could hear no heavy breathing. She heard no breathing at all!

Babe peeped out into the main cave and squealed in utmost horror. Standing there was, not Uncle Alton, but a massive caricature of a man: a huge thing like an irregular mud doll, clumsily made. It quivered and parts of it glistened and parts of it were dried and crumbly. Half of the lower left part of its face was gone, giving it a lopsided look. It had no perceptible mouth or nose, and its eyes were crooked, one higher than the other, both a dingy brown with no whites at all. It stood quite still looking at her, its only movement a steady unalive quivering.

It wondered about the queer little noise Babe had made.

Babe crept far back against a little pocket of stone, her brain running round and round in tiny circles of agony. She opened her mouth to cry out, and could not. Her eyes bulged and her face flamed with the strangling effort, and the two golden ropes of her braided hair twitched and twitched as she hunted hopelessly for a way out. If only she were out in the open—or in the wedge-shaped half-cave where the thing was—or home in bed!

The thing clumped toward her, expressionless, moving with a slow inevitability that was the sheer crux of horror. Babe lay wide-eyed and frozen, mounting pressure of terror stilling her lungs, making her heart shake the whole world. The monster came to the mouth of the little pocket, tried to walk to her and was stopped by the sides. It was such a narrow little fissure, and it was all Babe could do to get in. The thing from the wood stood straining against the rock at its shoulders, pressing harder and harder to get to Babe. She sat up slowly, so near to the thing that its odor was almost thick enough to see, and a wild hope burst through her voiceless fear. It couldn't get in! It couldn't get in because it was too big!

The substance of its feet spread slowly under the tremendous strain and at its shoulder appeared a slight crack. It widened as the monster unfeelingly crushed itself against the rock, and suddenly a large piece of the shoulder came away and the being twisted slushily three feet farther in. It lay quietly with its muddy eyes fixed on her, and then brought one thick arm up over its head and reached.

Babe scrambled in the inch farther she had believed impossible, and the filthy clubbed hand stroked down her back, leaving a trail of muck on the blue denim of the shirt she wore. The monster surged suddenly and, lying full length now, gained that last precious inch. A black hand seized one of her braids, and for Babe the lights went out.

When she came to, she was dangling by her hair from that same crusted paw. The thing held her high, so that her face and its featureless head were not more than a foot apart. It gazed at her with a mild curiosity in its eyes, and it swung her slowly back and forth. The agony of her pulled hair did what fear could not do— gave her a voice. She screamed. She opened her mouth and puffed up her powerful young lungs, and she sounded off. She held her throat in the position of the first scream, and her chest labored and pumped more air through her frozen throat. Shrill and monotonous and infinitely piercing, her screams.

The thing did not mind. It held her as she was, and watched. When it had learned all it could from this phenomenon, it dropped her jarringly, and looked around the half-cave, ignoring the stunned and huddled Babe. It reached over and picked up the leather brief case and tore it twice across as if it were tissue. It saw the sandwich Babe had left, picked it up, crushed it, dropped it.

Babe opened her eyes, saw that she was free, and just as the thing turned back to her she dove between its legs and out into the shallow pool in front of the rock, paddled across and hit the other bank screaming. A vicious little light of fury burned in her; she picked up a grapefruit-sized stone and hurled it with all her frenzied might. It flew low and fast, and struck squashily on the monster's ankle. The thing was just taking a step toward the water; the stone caught it off balance, and its unpracticed equilibrium could not save it. It tottered for a long, silent moment at the edge and then splashed into the stream. Without a second look Babe ran shrieking away.

Cory Drew was following the little gobs of mold that somehow indicated the path of the murderer, and he was nearby when he first heard her scream. He broke into a run, dropping his shotgun and holding the .32-40 ready to fire. He ran with such deadly panic in his heart that he ran right past the huge cleft rock and was a hundred yards past it before she burst out through the pool and ran up the bank. He had to run hard and fast to catch her, because anything behind her was that faceless horror in the cave, and she was living for the one idea of getting away from there. He caught her in his arms and swung her to him, and she screamed on and on and on.

Babe didn't see Cory at all, even when he held her and quieted her.

The monster lay in the water. It neither liked nor disliked this new element. It rested on the bottom, its massive head a foot beneath the surface, and it curiously considered the facts that it had garnered. There was the little humming noise of Babe's voice that sent the monster questing into the cave. There was the black material of the brief case that resisted so much more than green things when he tore it. There was the little two-legged one who sang and brought him near, and who screamed when he came. There was this new cold moving thing he had fallen into. It was washing his body away. That had never happened before. That was interesting. The monster decided to stay and observe this new thing. It felt no urge to save itself; it could only be curious.

The brook came laughing down out of its spring, ran down from its source beckoning to the sunbeams and embracing freshets and helpful brooklets. It shouted and played with streaming little roots, and nudged the minnows and pollywogs about in its tiny backwaters. It was a happy brook. When it came to the pool by the cloven rock it found the monster there, and plucked at it. It soaked the foul substances and smoothed and melted the molds, and the waters below the thing eddied darkly with its diluted matter. It was a thorough brook. It washed all it touched, persistently. Where it found filth, it removed filth; and if there were layer on layer of foulness, then layer by foul layer it was removed. It was a good brook. It did not mind the poison of the monster, but took it up and thinned it and spread it in little rings round rocks downstream, and let it drift to the rootlets of water plants, that they might grow greener and lovelier. And the monster melted.

"I am smaller," the thing thought. "That is interesting. I could not move now. And now this part of me which thinks is going, too. It will stop in just a moment, and drift away with the rest of the body. It will stop thinking and I will stop being, and that, too, is a very interesting thing."

So the monster melted and dirtied the water, and the water was clean again, washing and washing the skeleton that the monster had left. It was not very big, and there was a badly-healed knot on the left arm. The sunlight flickered on the triangular silver plate set into the pale skull, and the skeleton was very clean now. The brook laughed about it for an age.

They found the skeleton, six grimlipped men who came to find a killer. No one had believed Babe, when she told her story days later. It had to be days later because Babe had screamed for seven hours without stopping, and had lain like a dead child for a day. No one believed her at all, because her story was all about the bad fella, and they knew that the bad fella was simply a thing that her father had made up to frighten her with. But it was through her that the skeleton was found, and so the men at the bank sent a check to the Drews for more money than they had ever dreamed about. It was old Roger Kirk, sure enough, that skeleton, though it was found five miles from where he had died and sank into the forest floor where the hot molds builded around his skeleton and emerged—a monster.

So the Drews had a new barn and fine new livestock and they hired four men. But they didn't have Alton. And they didn't have Kimbo. And Babe screams at night and has grown very thin.

No one can change my conviction that there are among us people like "Face." Not necessarily people from his strange point of origin, but from many. The reasons these folk have for concealing themselves are more obvious than any they might have for self-advertisement. You do not attempt to alter what you see on your visits to a museum—or to a zoo...

Poker Face

We all had to get up early that morning, and we still hadn't sense enough to get up from around the poker table. We'd called in that funny little guy from the accounting department they called Face to make it a foursome with the three of us. It had been nip and tuck from nine o'clock on—he played a nice game of stud. But tonight there was no one lucky man, and when Harry jokingly bet a nickel on a pair of fours and Delehanty took him up on it, the game degenerated into penny-ante. After a while we forgot whose deal it was and sat around just batting the breeze.

"Screwy game," said Delehanty. "What's the use of squattin' here all this time just to break even? Must be your influence, Face. Never happened before. We generally hand all our money over to Jack after four deals. Hey, Jack?"

I grinned. "The game still owes me plenty, bud," I said. "But I think you're right about Face. I don't know if you noticed it, but damn if that winning didn't go right around behind the deal—me, you, Face, Harry, me again. If I won two, everyone else would win two."

Face raised an eyebrow ridge because he hadn't any

33

eyebrows. There wasn't anything particularly remark-able about his features, except that they were absolutely without hair. The others carried an a.m. stubble, but his face gleamed nakedly, half luminous. He'd been a last choice, but a pretty good one. He said little, watched everyone closely and casually, and seemed like a pretty nice guy. "Noticed that, did you?" he asked. His voice was a very full tenor.

"That's right," said Harry. "How about it, Face? What is this power you have over poker?"

"Oh, just one of those things you pick up," he said.

Delehanty laughed outright. "Listen at that," he said. "He's like the ol' mountain climber who saw a volcano erupting in the range he'd scaled the day be-fore. 'By damn,' he says, 'why can't I be careful where I spit?' "

Everybody laughed but Face. "You think it just hap-pened? Would you like to see it happen again?"

That stopped the hilarity. We looked at him queerly. Harry said, "What's the dope?"

"Play with chips," said Face. "No money, no hard feelings. If you like, I won't touch the cards. Just to make it easy, I'll put it this way. Deal our four hands of stud. Jack'll win the first with three threes. Dele-hanty next with three fours. Me next with three fives. Harry next with three sixes. Each three-spread will come out hearts, diamonds, clubs in that order. You, Delehanty, start the deal. Go on—shuffle them all you like."

Delehanty was a little popeyed. "You wouldn't want to make a little bet on that, would you?" he breathed.

"I would not. I don't want to take your money that way. It would be like picking pockets."

"You're bats, Face," I said. "There's so little chance of a shuffled deck coming out that way that you might as well call it impossible."

"Try it," said Face quietly.

Delehanty counted the cards carefully, shuffled at least fifteen times with his very efficient gambler's riffle, and dealt around quickly. The cards flapped down in front of me—a jack face down, a six, and then—three threes; hearts, diamonds, clubs, in that order. Nobody said anything for a long time.

Finally, "Jack's got it," Harry breathed.

"Let me see that deck," snapped Harry. He swept it up, spread it out in his hands. "Seems O.K.," he said slowly, and turned to Face.

"Your deal," said Face woodenly.

Harry dealt quickly. I said, "Delehanty's s'posed to be next with three fours—right?" Yeah—right! Three fours lay in front of Delehanty. It was too much—cards shouldn't act that way. Wordlessly I reached for the cards, gathered them up, pitched them back over my shoulder. "Break out a new deck," I said. "Your deal, Face."

"Let Delehanty deal for me," said Face.

Delehanty dealt again, clumsily this time, for his hands trembled. That didn't matter—there were still three fives smiling up at Face when he was through.

"Your deal," whispered Harry to me, and turned half away from the table.

I took up the cards. I spent three solid minutes shuffling them. I had Harry cut them and then cut them again myself and then passed them to Delehanty for another cut. I dealt four hands, and Harry's was the winning hand, with three sixes—hearts, diamonds, clubs.

Delehanty's eyes were almost as big now as his ears. He said, "Heaven. All. Might. Tea," and rested his chin in his hands. I thought he was going to cry or something.

"Well?" said Face.

"Were we playing poker with this guy?" Harry asked no one in particular.

When by a great deal of hard searching, I found my voice again, I asked Face, "Hey, do you do that just any time you feel like it, or does it come over you at odd moments?"

Face laughed. "Any time," he said. "Want to see a

really pretty one? Shuffle and deal out thirteen cards to each of us, face down. Then look them over."

I gave him a long look and began to shuffle. Then I dealt. I think we were all a little afraid to pick up our cards. I know that when I looked at mine I felt as if someone had belted me in the teeth with a night stick. I had thirteen cards, and they were all spades. I looked around the table. Delehanty had diamonds. Face had hearts. Harry had clubs.

You could have heard a bedbug sneeze in the room until Harry began saying, "Ah, no. Ah, no. Ah, no," quietly, over and over, as if he were trying to tell himself something.

"Can they all do things like that where you come from?" I asked, and Face nodded brightly.

"Can everyone walk where you come from?" he returned. "Or see, or hear, or think? Sure."

"Just where do you come from?" asked Harry.

"I don't know," said Face. "I only know how I came and I couldn't explain it to you."

"Why not?"

"How could you explain an internal-combustion engine to an Australian bushman?"

"You might try," said Delehanty, piqued. "We's pretty smart bushmen, we is."

"Yeah," I chimed in. "I'm willing to allow you the brains to do those card tricks of yours; you ought to have enough savvy to put over an idea or two."

"Oh—the cards. That was easy enough. I felt the cards as you shuffled them."

"You felt with my fingers?"

"That's right. Want proof? Jack, your head is itching a little on the right side, near the top, and you're too lazy to scratch it just yet. Harry's got a nail pushing into the third toe of his right foot—not very bad, but it's there. Well, what do you say?"

He was right. I scratched. Harry shuffled his feet and said, "O.K., but what has that got to do with arranging the cards that way? Suppose you did feel them with our hands—then what?"

Face put his elbows on the table. "As for arranging the cards, that was done in the shuffle. You grasp half of the deck in each hand, bend them, let them flip out from under your thumbs. If you can control the pressure of each thumb carefully enough, you can make the right cards fall into the right places. You all shuffled at least four times; that made it that much easier for me."

Delehanty was popeyed again, "How did you know which cards were supposed to go in which places?"

"Memorized their order, of course," said Face. "I've seen that done in theaters even by men like you."

"So've I," said Harry. "But you still haven't told us how you arranged the deal. If you'd done the shuffling I could see it, but—"

"But I *did* do the shuffling," said Face. "I controlled that pressure of your thumbs."

"How about the cuts?" Delehanty put in, finding that at last we had him on the run. "When Jack dealt he handed the pack to Harry and me both to be cut."

"I not only controlled those cuts," said Face calmly, "but I made you do it."

"Go way," said Delehanty aggressively. "Don't give us that. How're you going to make a man do anything you like?"

"Skeptical animal, aren't you?" grinned Face; and Delehanty rose slowly, walked around the table, caught Harry by the shoulders and kissed him on both cheeks. Harry almost fell off his chair. Delehanty stood there rockily, his eyes positively bulging. Suddenly he expectorated with great violence. "What the dirty so and forth made me do that?" he wanted to know.

"Chummy, ain't you?" grinned Harry through his surprise.

Face said, "Satisfied, Delehanty?"

Delehanty whirled on him. "Why you little—" His fury switched off like a light going out. "Right again, Face." He went over and sat down. I never saw that Irishman back down like that before.

"You made him do that?" I asked.

Face regarded me gravely. "You doubt it?"

We locked glances for a moment, and then my feet gathered under me. I had a perverse desire to get on all fours and bark like a dog. It seemed the most natural thing in the world. I said quickly, "Not at all, Face, not at all!" My feet relaxed.

"You're the damnedest fellow I ever saw," said Harry. "What kind of a man are you anyway?"

"Just a plain ordinary man with a job," said Face, and looked at Delehanty.

"So am I," said Harry, "but I can't make cards sit up and typewrite, or dumb Irishers snuggle up to their fellowmen."

"Don't let that bother you," said Face. "I told you before—there's nothing more remarkable in that than there is in walking, or seeing, or hearing. I was born with it, that's all."

"You said everyone was, where you come from," Harry reminded him. "Now spill it. Just where did you come from?"

"Geographically," said Face, "not very far from here. Chronologically, a hell of a way."

Harry looked over my way blankly. "Now what does all that mean?"

"As near as I can figure out," said Face, "It means just what I said. I come from right around here—fifty miles, maybe—but the place I came from is thirty-odd thousand years away."

"Years *away*?" I asked, by this time incapable of being surprised. "You mean 'ago,' don't you?"

"Away," repeated Face. "I came along duration, not through time itself."

"Sounds very nice," murmured Delehanty to a royal flush he had thumbed out for himself.

Face laughed. "Duration isn't time—it parallels it. Duration is a dimension. A dimension is essentially a measurement along a plane of existence. By that I mean that any given object has four dimensions, and these extend finitely, along four planes—length, width, height, duration. The last is no different from the others; nor is it any less tangible. You simply take it for granted.

"When you're ordering a piece of lumber, for instance, you name its measurements. You say you want a two by six, twelve feet long. You don't order its duration; you simply take for granted it will extend long enough in that dimension to suit your needs. You would build better if you measured it as carefully as you do the others, but your life span is too short for you to care that much."

"I think I savvy that," said Harry, who had been following carefully, "but what do you mean by saying that you came 'along' duration?"

"Again, just what I said. You can't move without moving along the plane of dimension. If you walk down the street, you move along its length. If you go up in an elevator, you move along its height. I came along duration."

"You mean you projected yourself into the fourth dimension?" asked Harry.

"No!" said Face violently, and snorted. "I told you—duration is a dimension, not another set of dimensions. Can you project yourself into length, or height, or into any one dimension? Of course not! The four are interdependent. That fourth-dimensional stuff you read is poppycock. There's no mystery about the fourth dimension. It isn't an impalpable word. It's a basis of measurement."

I said, "What's this business of your traveling along it?"

Face spread out his hands. "As I said before, duration is finite. Suppose you wanted to walk from Third Street to Fifth Street. First you'd locate a sidewalk that would take you in the direction you were going. You'd follow that until it ended. Then you'd locate one that would take you to your destination. Where the one stopped and the other started is Fourth Street. Now if you want to go twenty blocks instead of two, you simply repeat that process until you get where you're going.

"Traveling along duration is exactly the same thing.

Just as you enter a street at a certain point in its length, so you encounter an object on the street at a certain point in its duration. Maybe it's near the beginning, maybe near the end. You follow it along that dimension—you don't project yourself into it. All objects have two terminations in duration—inception and destruction. You travel along an object's duration until it ceases to exist beside you because you have reached the end of it—or the beginning. Then you proceed to find another object so that you may continue in the same direction, exactly as you proceeded to find yourself another sidewalk in your little trek across town."

"I'll be damned," said Delehanty. "I can understand it!"

"Me, too," Harry said. "That much of it. But exactly how did you travel along duration? I can get the idea of walking beside a building's length, for instance, but I can't see myself walking along beside … er … how long it lasted, if you see what I mean. Or do *I* see what I mean?"

"Now you're getting to something that may be a little tough to explain," said Face. "You have few expressions in your language that could cover it. About the clearest way for me to put it is this: My ability to travel in that particular direction is the result of my ability to perceive it. If you could only perceive two dimensions, length and breadth, you would be completely in the dark about the source of an object which dropped on you from above. If you couldn't sense the distance from here to the door—if you didn't know the door existed, nor the distance to it, you wouldn't be able to make the trip. I can see along duration as readily as you can see up and down a road. I can move along it equally readily."

"Do you stay in one place while you travel duration?" I asked suddenly.

"I can. I don't have to, though. You can go forward and upward while you curve to the left, can't you? Mix 'em anyway you like."

Harry piped up. "You say you came thirty thousand

years. How is that possible? You don't look as if you're much older than I am."

"I'm not," said Face, "in point of years existed. That is, I didn't live those years. I—passed them."

"How long did it take you?"

Face smiled. "Your question is ridiculous, Harry. 'How long' is a 'durational' term. It involves passage of time, which is a convenient falsehood. Time is static, objects mobile. I can't explain a true state of affairs from the basis of a false conception."

Harry shut up. I asked him something that had been bothering me. "Where did you come from, Face, and—why?"

He looked at me deeply, that eyebrow ridge rising a trifle. "I came—I was sent. I came because I was qualified for the job, I was sent because—well, someone had to be sent, to restore the balance of the city."

"What city?"

"I don't know. It had a name, I suppose, but it was forgotten. There was no need for a name. Do you name your toothbrush, or your bed sheets, or anything else that has been nearly part of you all your life? No one ever left the city, no one ever arrived at it. There were other cities, but no one cared about them, where they were, who their people were and what they were like, and so on. There was no need to know. The city was independent and utterly self-sufficient. It was the ultimate government. It was not a democracy, for each individual was subjugated entirely to the city. But it was not a dictatorship as you know the term, for it had no dictators. It had no governing body, as a matter of fact. It didn't need one. It had no laws but those of habit and custom. It ran smoothly because all of its internal frictions had been worn smooth by the action of the centuries. It was an anarchistic society in the true sense of anarchism—society without need of government."

"That's an impossibility," said Harry, who had a reputation as a minor barroom sociologist.

"I came from that city," Face reminded him gently. "Why is it impossible? You must take certain things into account before you make such rash statements. Your human nature is against such an organization. Your people would be like lost sheep—possibly like lost wolverines—under such a set-up. But my people were not like that—not after centuries of breeding for the most desirable traits, living circumscribed ways of life, thinking stereotyped thoughts. Imagine it if you can.

"Now the city was divided into two halves, like the halves of a great brain. For every death there was a birth; for every loss there was a gain or an equal loss on the other side. The equation was kept balanced, the scales level. The city was permanent, inexorable, immortal and static."

"What did they do with their spare time?" asked Harry.

"They lay in their cubicles until they were needed."

"Were there no theaters, ball games—nothing like that?" asked Delehanty.

Face shook his head. "Amusement is for the relaxation of an imperfect mind," he said. "A mind that has been trained to do one thing and one thing only needs no stimulation or change of pace."

"Why was the city so big?" asked Harry. "Good gosh, a civilization like that doesn't *mean* anything. Why didn't it simply degenerate into the machines that ruled it? Why keep all those humans if they must live like machines?"

Face shrugged. "When the city was instituted, there was a population of that size to allow for. Then, it had a rigid human government, and there was crime and punishment and pain and happiness. They were disposed of in a few generations—they were not logical, you see, and the city was designed on the philosophy that what is not logical is also not necessary. By that time the city was too steeped in its own traditions; there was no one left to make such a radical change as to cut down on the population. The city could care for that many—likewise it could not exist as it was unless it did care for that many. Many human offices were disposed of as they became unnecessary and automatic. One of these was that of controller of population. The machines took care of that—they and the unbreakable customs."

"Hell!" said Delehanty explosively. "I wouldn't go for that. Why didn't the people push the whole thing over and get some fun out of life?"

"They didn't want it!" said Face, as if he were repeating a self-evident fact, and was surprised that he had to. "They had never had that sort of life; they never heard or read or saw anything of the sort. They had no more desire to do things like that than you have to play pattycake! They weren't constituted to enjoy it."

"You still haven't told us why you left the place," I reminded him.

"I was coming to that. In the city there was a necessity for the pursuance of certain knowledges, as a safety measure against the time when one or another of the machines might need rebuilding by a man who understood them.

"One of these men was an antiquarian named Hark Vegas, which is really not a name at all but a combination of sounds indicating a number. His field was history—the development of all about him, from its earliest recorded mythologies and beyond that to its most logical sources. In the interests of the city, he so applied himself to his work that he uncovered certain imponderables—historical trends which were neither logical nor in harmony with the records. They were of no importance, perhaps, but their existence interfered with the perfection of his understanding. The only way he could untangle these unimportant matters was to investigate them personally. And so—that is what he did.

"He waited until his successor was thoroughly trained, so that in any eventuality the city would not be left without an antiquarian for more than a very little while, and he studied carefully the records of the city's customs. These forbade any citizen's leaving the city, and carefully described the boundaries thereof. They were so very old, however, that they neglected to stipulate the boundaries along the duration dimension, since duration perception was a development of only the past four or five thousand years. As an antiquarian, Hark Vegas was familiar with the technique. He moved himself out along the duration of a metallic fragment and thus disappeared from the city.

"Now this unheard-of happening disturbed the timeless balance of the city, for Hark Vegas was nowhere to be found. Within seconds of his disappearance, news of it had reached the other half of the city, and the group of specialists there.

"The matter involved me immediately for several reasons. In the first place, my field was—damn it, there's no word for it in your language yet. It's a mental science and has to do with time perceptions. At any rate, I was the only one whose field enabled him to reason where Hark Vegas had gone. Secondly, Hark Vegas was my contemporary in the other half of the city. We would both be replaced within a week, but during that week there would be one too many in my half of the city, one too few in his—an intolerable, absolutely unprecedented state of affairs. There was only one thing to do, since I was qualified, and that was to find him and bring him back. My leaving would restore the balance; if I were successful in finding him, our return would not disturb it. It was the only thing to do, for the status quo had to be maintained at all costs. I acquired a piece of the metal he had used—an easy thing to do, since everything in the city was catalogued—and came away."

Face paused to light a cigarette. The man smoked, I had noticed, with more sheer enjoyment than anyone I had ever met.

"Well," said Harry impatiently, "did you find him?"

Face leaned back in a cloud of blue smoke and stared dreamily at the ceiling. "No," he said. "And I'll tell you why.

"I ran into a characteristic of dimensions that was so utterly simple that it had all but escaped me. Let me give you an example. How many sides has a cube?"

"Six," said Harry promptly.

Face nodded. "Exactly. Excluding the duration di-mension, the cube is a three-dimensional body and has six sides. There are *two* sides as manifestations of each dimension. I think I overlooked that. You see, there are four dimensions, but eight—*directions!*"

He paused, while the three of us knotted our brows over the conception. "Right and left," he said. "Up and down. Forward and backward—and 'beginningwards' and 'endwards'—the two directions in the duration di-mension!"

Delehanty raised his head slowly. "You mean you—didn't know which *way* to go?"

"Precisely. I entered the durational field and struck off blindly in the wrong direction! I went as far as I reasoned Hark Vegas had gone, and then stopped to look around. I found myself in such a bewildering, uproarious, chaotic world that I simply hadn't the men-tal equipment to cope with it. I had to retreat into a deserted place and develop it. I came into your world—here, about eight years ago. And when I had begun to get the ways of this world, I came out of hid-ing and began my search. It ended almost as soon as it had begun, for I stopped searching!

"Do you know what happened to me? Do you real-ize that never before had I seen color, or movement, or argument, or love, hate, noise, confusion, growth, death, laughter? Can you imagine my delighted first glimpses of a street fight, a traffic jam, a factory strike? I should have been horrified, perhaps—but never had I seen such beautiful marvels, such superb and profound and moving happenings. I threw myself into it. I became one of you. I became an accountant, throttling down what powers I alone of all this earth possess, striving for life as a man on an equal footing with the rest of men. You can't know my joy and my delight! I make a mistake in my entries, and the city—this city, does not care or suffer for it, but brawls on unheeding. My responsibilities are to myself alone, and I defy my cast-steel customs and laugh doing it. I'm living here, you see? Living! Go back? Hah!"

"Colors," I murmured. "Noise, and happy filth, and sorrows and screams. So they got you—*too!*"

Face's smile grew slowly and then flashed away. He stared at me like some alabaster-faced statue for nearly a full minute, and then the agile tendrils of his mind whipped out and encountered mine. We clutched each other thus, and the aura of our own forces around us struck two men dumb.

"Hark Vegas," he said woodenly.

I nodded.

He straightened, drew a deep breath, threw back his head and laughed. "This colossal joke," he said, wiping his eyes, "was thirty-eight thousand years in the making. Pleased to meet you—Jack."

We left then. Harry and Delehanty can't remember anything but a poker game.

This opus, sheer "space-opera," is included here primarily because with it I can modestly take my place among the prognosticators. Based on the problem of isotope separation, it was written three years before the organization of the Manhattan Project, Major Groves' brain trust tried five methods to accomplish the trick of separating U-235 from U-238, in a mass of metal which was all chemically pure uranium. Here's one they never thought of . . .

Artnan Process

Slimmy Cob and his hair stood up short, tough and wiry. His eyes were slitted like his mouth, both emitting, from his dark face, thin lines of blue-white. "Blow!" he gritted, and his finger tightened on the trigger of the snub-nosed weapon he held.

The other man in the ship raised his face by making his pillar of neck disappear into great hunched shoulders. I was afraid of this, he thought, and his fingers froze over the control panel. "Better put that toy away," he said softly.

"I want a chance to unload it," said Slimmy, and he moved the muzzle coldly across the back of Bell Bellew's hairless skull. "And I'll sure get my chance unless you get out of that bucket seat and let me land the ship. Ain't kiddin', son."

Bell grinned tightly, jammed his knees into the recesses provided for them under the board, and with one dazzling movement threw two switches. The gravity plates under Slimmy's feet went dead and those in the overhead whipped the little man upward. He hung there, spitting and swearing like an angry kitten. Wrenching one pinned arm away, he aimed and fired. An opaque white liquid squirted downward, lathering the big man's skull, running down over his ears and eyes, down his neck. Bell swore chokingly, clawing at his face. He felt swiftly over the panel, his practiced fingers finding the right switches as if they were tipped with eyes. Slimmy fell heavily to the deck plates, and Bell pounced on him.

Great fingers wrapped themselves around Slimmy's throat, through which gasped the words, "Dammit! Why didn't I try to kill you outright instead of poisoning you?" His jaws clamped, and his slot of a mouth closed as his slitted eyes opened wide and began to pop.

On the arid, shining planet below the silver ship, three naked, leather-skinned Martians crouched around a compact recording instrument, their implacably logical minds cubbyholing the above happenings. Their recorder, receiving by means of a tight beam vibration from the control room of the Earthlings' ship, showed in its screen every detail of the chamber, clearly sounded every word. A slight drift of the ship above moved it away from the spy beam, and the signals faded out. One of the Martians bent swiftly to the instrument while the others spoke in their high, monotonous voices.

"They are unaccountable as ever," said the first. His words were spoken syllable by syllable, with no emphasis on any of them, with no rise or fall of tone at the end of his sentence. The language of Mars is necessarily that way, since Martians are tone-deaf.

"It is beyond understanding," said the other, "that these two humans, who have come from the Solar System to this planet of Procyon, should have lived so amicably together until the day they arrive here on Artna, and then strive to kill one another."

"At least," said the first, "we have discovered their purpose in coming here."

"Yes. I trust that they will meet with no success."

"If they fail, they will have done no more than we have. The Artnans are far from hostile, but guard their secret closely. However, it seems reasonable to me to dispatch these Earthmen. Their presence here accomplishes nothing for us."

The third Martian turned the still-dead recording machine at this. "I would advise against that," he piped. "He," by the way, is a term of convenience. Martians are parthenogenetic, or self-germinating females. Variation of racial strains is accomplished by a periodic mutual absorption. "Earthmen, involved and unnecessary as their thought-processes are, have achieved a certain degree of development. Hampered by such inefficient and wandering mentalities, they could only have developed so far by possessing some unexplained influence over the laws of chance. Should that quality be used here, they might discover the secret we are after—how the Artnans produce U-235 so cheaply that they can undersell Martian and Terrestrial atomic fuel."

"There is reason in that," said the first Martian, than which there is no higher compliment to a Martian. "If we cannot discover the secret ourselves, we may conceivably secure it from any who get it before us." He turned back to his machine, but to no avail. The little silver ship had disappeared over the horizon, and the Martian spy ray was strictly a sight-line proposition.

When the blue began to show through Slimmy's tanned skin, Bell Bellew let go the little man's throat, took one wizened ear between each great forefinger and thumb, and began to rap on the deck plates with Slimmy's skull. A little of this, and the gun toter called it quits. Bell sat on his prostrate shipmate and grinned broadly.

"Get off," wheezed Slimmy. "I feel all crummy, lying under this big pile of—"

Bell put a hand under his chin and slammed the wiry head on the deck again.

"O.K.—O.K. You got me. Now what?"

"What was it you loaded that gun with?" asked Bill.

"Zinc stearate, lug, in an emulsion of carbohydrates and hydrogen oxide. I couldn't think of anything you needed more or liked less."

"Soap and water," nodded Bell. "Couldn't believe it, that's all, coming from you." He climbed off. "Enough horseplay, little one. We got to get to work. We're over the horizon, anyway. That spy ray of theirs won't see any more of this dray-ma."

Slimmy got his feet under him uncertainly, and shook his spinning head. "Now that we're here, what do we do?"

"We land as near as we can get to the Artnan's transmutation plant and see if we can get a gander how to make U-235 out of U-238."

"You really believe they can do that?"

"They must. I used to think they mined it, but they don't. Artna has an atmosphere much like Earth's, except that there's more xenon and neon and less nitrogen in the air. Also considerable water; and you know as well as I do that '235 can't exist where there's water."

"I dunno," said Slimmy. "The fact that they produce so much, so cheaply, is a contradiction in terms. Uranium is a little more plentiful here than it is on Earth, but it has less than Mars. And the ratio of '238 to '235 is 140 to 1, same as anywhere else. Damn, boy," he burst out suddenly, "won't it be something if we crack this racket?"

"Sure will," breathed Bell.

The simple words bore a weight of profound meaning, for in spite of their skylarking tendencies, Cob and Bellew never belittled the importance of their mission. Its history went back nearly five hundred years, to the ill-fated days when Earth first flung her pioneer ships out into space, to bring back their tales of other, older civilizations. They found the dead remains of titans of Jupiter, and they brought back miles of visigraph records from the steaming swamps of Venus. But from Mars they brought undreamed-of power; a beam of broadcast energy from the old red planet that seemed inexhaustible. Earthmen were free to come and go; Earthmen saw the broadcasting towers that gave them their power, and the measureless stores of purest U-235 that fed it. The only thing they were not allowed to see was the plant which supplied the '235. Earth did not care much about that—why should they? They got power from Mars for a fraction of what it cost them to produce it themselves, so they took Martian power and shut down their own plants.

Of course, there were one or two small rights which the Martians exacted in exchange—little matters concerning the right to Earth's mineral resources, occasional requests to the effect that Earthmen must stop researches in certain directions, must prevent the publication of certain books, must limit their travel in certain directions . . . The edicts came far apart, and were applied with gentle and efficient firmness. Occasionally a group of Earthy hotheads would find reason to resent the increasing Martian influence. They were disciplined, usually by the greater mass of their own race, the hypnotized sheep who blathered of "beneficent dictatorship"; quoted interminably the Mars-schooled leader of men who burned his speeches into the souls of all—Hyatte Grove, who said, "To Mars we owe our power, our transportation, our every industry. To Mars we owe our daily bread, our warless, uneventful, steadily progressive lives. The Martian power beam is the beating heart of our world."

Earthmen outnumbered Martians ten to one. Martians outlived Earthmen eight to one. The advantage was with Mars. The Martian conquest was applied without blood, without pain. There was no war of worlds, no great fleet of ray-equipped ships. There was just the warming, friendly power beam, and the great generosity of Earth's "Elder Sister." Generation after generation of men lived and died, and each of them was gradually led deeper into the slowspun web of the red planet. Earth entered into a new era, one of passive peace, submission, slavery.

Some men knew it for what it was, and did not care. Some cared, but could think of nothing to do about it. Some did something about it, and were quietly killed. Most of humanity didn't bother about what happened. You were born and cared for. You grew up and were given a job. You were comfortable. Sometimes you were allowed to marry and have children, if it was all right with Mars. Married or single, there was room for everyone. When you were too old to be useful, you begged and were cared for by your fellows—that was easy, for everyone had so much. Then you died, and they dropped your carcass into the disintegrating furnaces. So what difference could it make whether or not man or Martian ran the show?

When man owned the Earth, you were told, he made a mess of it. No one killed now, or stole or broke any law. It was better. No one thought very deeply or clearly; no one had ambition, pride, freedom. That was better, too—for Mars. Mars grew fat on Earth's endeavor.

But some Earthmen didn't know when they were well off. They read the forbidden books, and studied the forbidden sciences, and most of them were killed off before they could add anything; but some did, and in a few centuries they had accomplished something. They knew these things:

Earth had a soul of her own, and they were determined to restore it to her.

Mars was the master—but Mars herself was a slave!

And power had enslaved the red planet even as it had Earth. A thousand years and more before the first clumsy Earth ships had landed on Mars, Mars, too, had had great plants for the transmutation of '238 into '235. But one night an object was found on the Great Plain near the city of Lanamarn. It had appeared without a whisper; it was an irregular cylinder containing various simple objects—spheres, cubes, triangular and square plane surfaces of a tough alloy. Each was marked by a symbol. The Martians experimented with the things, drew some shrewd conclusions, and deposited other objects in the cylinder, replacing the cap. There was a shrill whine; on removing the cap again, the Martians found that their offerings had disappeared and were replaced by still other objects, each of which also bore a symbol.

After long and painstaking efforts, a written language was established between Mars and the mystery from space which had sent the cylinder. The Martians learned that it had come from Artna, a planet of the Procyon system, and that the method of transmission was by way of the probability wave, a scientific refinement beyond the understanding even of Mars. It worked on the principle that matter cannot be destroyed; if it *is* annihilated in one portion of space, it must necessarily appear somewhere else. The transmission is instantaneous; as soon as it is negated at its source, it simply occurs at its destination.

And the Artnans had a proposition, to wit: Perhaps there was some little thing the Martians would like in return for the boron which showed up so strongly on the Artnan's teleospectrographs. The Martians sent out a sample of U-238 and asked if the Artnans could transmute it, in bulk, to U-235. The Artnans could, and did. They cheerfully sent plans for the construction of a tremendous plant on the plain. U-238 was dumped into hoppers, stored by machinery in bins deep in the heart of the apparatus, and disappeared. Elsewhere in the plant pure '235 poured out in pulverized, greenish-black abundance.

So Martian transmutation plants shut down, and Mars used Artnan atomic fuel exclusively. While boron was cheap, the arrangement was greatly to Mars' advantage. But the Artnans easily realized their advantage when they had cornered the power market, and they jumped the price. They kept it at just the level that would make it impossible for the Martians to reopen their own plants, until they had nearly exhausted the Martians' supply of both uranium and boron. They would accept no substitute for the boron; Mars faced an extreme economic reversal when the fortunate fact of communications with Earth was established. Hence Mars' economic penetration of Earth's resources; and now, Mars could afford to sit back and enjoy her position. Earthmen slaved in the boron mines; cargo after cargo of Terrestrial uranium was freighted to Mars to feed the maw of the gigantic "transmutation" plant on the Great Plain.

All this was discovered by Earth's spies, the dozens who came back out of the hundreds of thousands that sought the information. In two centuries, nine attempts were made on Earth to design and build a ship which could travel to Procyon fast enough to spare its crew the misfortune of dying of old age before the ship reached there. Eight crews of workers were discovered and killed or dispersed, put to work in the mines by wandering, gently thorough Martian investigators. The ninth ship got away—a physical impossibility, as the Mars-hating element on Earth freely admitted. Mars gave them no permission to build and launch the little silver craft; but the Martian investigators stretched the probability and did not discover the hidden factory.

Perhaps it was purposeful. Perhaps Mars was curious to know whether Earthmen could find the secret of Artnan transmutation. Mars couldn't. Even now that they had Earth's vast resources at their disposal, the Martians would be happy to free themselves from the Artnan monopoly of transmutation. They remembered with bitterness the carefully outfitted body of operatives who had entered the transmission chamber and had gone to Artna via the wave, in place of a scheduled cargo of boron. The Artnans, with their next shipment of '235, included the six-legged, two-foot-long body of an Artnan and a polite note thanking the Martians for the inclusion of the *corpses!* and expressing regret that no living thing could traverse space time via the wave; also a reminder that the latest boron shipment was slightly overdue.

All of which flashed through Bell Bellew's mind as he stood beside Slimmy Cob and stared down at Artna. It had been a long trip—three years or so, even with the slight space warp stolen by workers in Martian shipyards. But Slimmy was good company, even if he did prefer horsing around to anything else in the world. They had both been picked for that quality, among many others. The reason was that the Martian mind is completely without humor, and the less Martians could understand the two men, the better it would be.

"Do you see what I see?" asked Slimmy after a long moment.

Bell followed the little man's pointing finger. Down in a hollow, nearly invisible from above, lay the squat shape of the Martian space cruiser.

"I do. I wouldn't worry about that, Slimmy. I expected that they'd be here."

"Why?"

"As I told you—I don't think it was just luck that got this ship off Earth, out of our system. I think the Martians let us."

"Yeah." There was that disbelief in Slimmy's voice. "The Martians have always treated us that way—let us do as we pleased, when we pleased. Wipe the rest of that soap off, Bell; it's addled your brain."

Bellew gave Slimmy a playful pat that brought him up against the opposite bulkhead, and went back to the controls. "Let me know when you sight anything that looks like the Great Plain transmutation plant," he said. "We can start from there."

The planet was but slightly larger than Earth, with an astonishingly smooth topography. There were no mountain ranges, and yet there were no true plains. The whole planet was surfaced with small rolling hillocks. Most were sandy; there was little vegetation. The Artnans, whose metabolism was a mineral one, had no agriculture.

After an hour or two Slimmy grunted and came away from the forward observation port and switched on the visiplate, tuning in the buildings he had spotted. "There she be, cap'n," he said.

Bell studied the great pile of alloy. "You got to give credit to those Martians," he said. "They certainly built theirs the spit an' image of this one."

"Not quite," said Slimmy, swinging the range finders. "Look there—see that . . . that—What is it, anyway?"

"Sort of a shed," said Bell. "One flat building, not more than three feet high, and all of ten miles square!"

A warning signal pinged, and their eyes swiveled toward it. A yellow light blinked among the studs on the panel. "Vibrations," gritted Bell, and put a thousand feet of altitude under them so fast that he heard Slimmy's kneecaps crackle. They circled slowly over the shed, feeling carefully ahead of them with delicate instruments, and charted the hemisphere of tight-knit waves that roofed the flat structure.

"What is it?" asked Slimmy.

"Dunno. Let's sit down and see if we can find out."

The ship settled down gently, her antigrav plates moaning. Bell followed the curve of the vibration field at a safe distance, and came down in a depression a hundred yards from its invisible edge.

"Air O.K.?"

"Sure," said Slimmy. "Just like home. Temperature's just under blood heat. Come a-walkin'!"

They strapped on side arms and went out, using the air lock for safety's sake. They topped a rise and stood a moment looking at the shed. It was barely visible from the ground, and there wasn't a sign of life anywhere about.

"Wonder why the sand don't drift over the thing," said Slimmy.

"This might be why," Bell grunted. He was staring at a line in the sand across the path. On their side of it, the sand puffed and tumbled in the light breeze. Toward the shed, however, there was apparently no moving air. "See that line? Unless I'm 'way off my base, that's the edge of the vibration field." He scooped up a handful of sand, stepped cautiously close to the line and tossed it. The sand fanned out, drifted over the line and—disappeared.

Slimmy tried it for himself before he commented. "I would gather," he said dryly, "that the Artnans would rather not have anyone look into that shed."

"Something like that," said Bell. "Look!" The crest of a nearby dune detached itself and scrabbled on six scrawny legs toward the line. It shot between the startled Earthmen, over the line, almost to the low wall of the shed before it turned up its pointed tail and burrowed quickly under the sand.

"What was that?" asked Slimmy.

"An Artnan, from what I've heard."

"Nasty little critter," said Slimmy. "Hey—the field didn't seem to bother it any, Bell."

"So I noticed. Seems that the field has been set up for the benefit of you and me. And maybe even for our Martian friends over there."

As they turned back toward their ship, Slimmy said pensively, "What we just saw is justification for the Laidlaw Hypothesis, if it makes any difference to you."

"What do you mean?"

"Speaks for itself, doesn't it? Laidlaw said that the inhabitants of any Solar System have a mutual ancestor, parallel evolutions, and similar metabolisms. You know yourself that Martians, Earthmen, Venusians and the extinct Jovians are all bipeds composed mainly of hydrocarbons. That field was set up to keep such molecular structures out. The sand here is apparently something of the sort. The Artnan who ran through the field was something different. We'll catch us one sometime and find out just what makes him tick."

"Yeah. You got something there. What interests me,

though, is what's in that shed. If we guessed right about who it was put up for, then the shed must cover something they want to keep Solar noses out of. Ah—it wouldn't by any chance be what we're looking for, would it?"

Slimmy's eyes glowed. "The transmutation plant? Could be, pal; could be. It's adjacent to the Prob.-wave transmitter. It's screened against Earth or Martian interference."

"Huh!" Bell ran a thick forefinger up behind his ear. "We got a problem here, little man. We toss ourselves through nine-odd light years of space and wind up flat-footed in front of a killer-wave thrown up around a cubist's idea of a beanfield. I sort of expected a city—machinery, people, maybe."

"It's not simple," said Slimmy. "Howsoever, let's see if you can make your brains go where your flat feet fear to tread. Let's go to work on the Martians. From the looks of things, they've been messing around here for quite some time."

"Want to go right to work, don't you?" grinned Bell. "Always wanted to get a Martian alone away from his playmates so you could tie a half hitch in his eye stalks! O.K., buddy—where do we find us one?"

"If I know Martians, there ought to be a couple sniffing around our ship by this time."

There were.

They were lined up in front of the air lock, their spare bodies quivering with the palpitation peculiar to their race, and with their eye stalks pointing rigidly toward the approaching Earthmen, points together, in the well-known Martian cross-eyed stare. They had, of course, sensed the body vibrations of the men quite some time ago; the very fact that they were there meant that they were ready for a showdown.

"Hi, fellers," said Slimmy laconically, flipping the butt of his atomic gun to make sure that it was loose in the holster.

"What are you doing here?" piped the Martian on the right.

"We're rick-bijitting for a dew-jaw," said Slimmy immediately.

He had studied the masterworks of the ancients in his extreme youth.

"Yes," said Bell, taking the cue. "We willised the altibob, and no sooner did we jellik than—*boom!* here we are."

The Martians regarded them silently. "You do not tell the truth," one of them said.

"It ain't a lie," Bell dead-panned.

The evasion served its purpose, for to them, anything that was not a lie was the truth, and vice versa. Their hearing apparatus was partly sensitive to air-vibration and partly telepathic. Bell's last statement was the truth and they knew it was the truth; that convinced them. They'd die before they admitted they didn't know what the men were talking about.

"What are *you* doing here?" Slimmy countered, before their machinelike minds could work on the problem.

The Martians stiffened. "It is not for you to ask," said one of them.

"Aw, don't be like that, son," drawled Bell. "Haven't Martians always told Earthmen that Mars takes only its just due, and does nothing for Earth but good?"

"Yeah," said Slimmy. His inflection was drawn-out, lowering, and meant "That's a lot of so-and-so!"

But to the Martians "Yeah" meant "Yes," and that was that. "Why should things be different here? You don't have to hide the fact that you're looking for the same thing we are; maybe we can make a little deal."

"Sure—come in and set awhile!" Bell pushed past the Martians and unlatched the air lock. He knew that turning his back on the enemy was bad tactics, but it was good diplomacy. Besides, fast on their feet as Martians were, no one in the Universe could draw, aim and fire faster than little Slimmy Cob.

Slimmy walked around the Martians, not between them, and sidled into the ship. He apparently faced the Martians merely to talk to them. "Sure—come on in.

Maybe we can give each other a hand. We can decide later what to do if we get the information we're after."

Three sets of eye stalks intertwined briefly, and then the three spindly Martians bent and entered the silver ship.

The Martians squatted in a row against the starboard bulkhead, sipping Earth's legendary cocola through glassite straws and coming as near to a feeling of well-being as was possible to these unemotional logicians. Slimmy's sharp eyes had noticed that one of them was taller than the others, the second taller than the third. Knowing that Martian names, being in the semi-telepathic Martian language, were unpronounceable to humans, he had dubbed them Heaven, Its Wonders, and Hell.

"Have another coke," said Bell heartily.

Its Wonders passed his empty flask. Bellew flashed a glance at Slimmy and Slimmy nodded. The Martians were getting nicely mellow; a carbonated drink plasters up the Martian metabolism with amazing efficiency. Intoxication, however, is not befuddlement to a Martian. It merely makes him move slower and think faster. If he drinks enough, he will stop altogether and turn into a genius for an hour or so. The idea of gassing the Martians up was to disarm them as to the human's motives; for they knew that no human would dare to try to pull the wool over a drunken Martian's eyes.

The Martians accepted the drink as a gesture of good faith, for they knew that they would soon be unable to navigate. It was the pipe of peace between them, with the Earthmen paying the piper, which was the way any deal with Mars seems to work out. So when the pale-blue flush began to blossom across their leathery hides, Slimmy went to work on them.

"Look fellers," he said bluntly, "there's no sense in our cutting each other's throats for a while yet. If you've guessed what we're here after, you've probably guessed right. We know that Martian '238 isn't transmuted into '235 on Mars. We know it's done here, in that flat building under the killer field over there. All we want to know is how it's done, and whether or not the method can be used in our System."

"What has that to do with us?" asked Hell.

"I'll take the question as a feeler," Bellew cut it. "You want to find out how much else we know. All right. We know that more than half of Terrestrial and Martian industry is being diverted to the production of boron to pay for the Artnan's processing of '238. We know that Martian domina... er ... control of the Solar System won't be complete unless and until the Artnan process of transmutation is made the property of Mars; for every indication shows that the cost of the Artnan process must be practically nothing. We know that the Martian Command did not have the process when we left the System three years ago, and we know that you don't have it yet because we wouldn't have found any Martians here if you had."

Heaven said, "What do you want to find the process for?"

"I might say that we of Earth would like to return to Mars some of the many kindnesses she has done us," said Slimmy around the tongue of his cheek. "And I might say that it's none of your damn business. I'll do neither, and simply say that I won't insult your intelligence by considering the question."

Three sets of eye stalks fumblingly sought each other out and intertwining, connected their owners in a swift, silent conference. Coming out of the huddle, Heaven addressed the humans. "We have certain information bearing on the matter in hand. How can we be assured that it will be to our benefit to share it?"

Bell answered that. "I've no idea how long you've been here, but it seems as though you haven't got on the right track yet. I don't know whether we'll be able to find the process with your information and our brains. If we can, well and good. If we can't, what have you lost?"

"We will share it," decided Its Wonders instantly. "All we know is this: The Artnans are a race totally unlike anything in our System. They have a mineral metabolism, feeding on ores and excreting sulphides. Their culture is beyond our understanding; they seem beyond the reach of the Solar reasoning. They have made no attempt to drive us away from the planet. They have also made no attempt to communicate with us, in spite of the fact that they must know we are Martians and that it is with Martians that they trade. The vibration field around the transmutation plant cannot be penetrated by anything but light; it even excludes a spy ray. There is no way of estimating the extent of their science or their civilization. They exist mainly underground; for all we know, this may be an artificial planet. There is a possibility that their science is no more advanced than ours, but that it has simply progressed along other lines. The trade with Mars may be a major or a very minor industry with them. It is completely impossible to tell. That is all we have been able to discover."

"That might help," said Bellew, "and it might not. We'll work on it. Now. There's one more little point we have to take care of. How can all concerned be sure that there is no dirty work? How do we know that we will not be killed if we get the secret; how do you know that we will not kill you for it if you beat us to the gun?"

"We can promise," said Its Wonders in his spark-coil voice.

"Won't do, chum," said Slimmy. "No reflection on you, but in spite of the fact that a Martian has never been known to break his word, we don't want you establishing precedents. Bad for the racial morale. Got any other ideas?"

Bellew sometimes wished that Martians could add inflection, voice control, to their speech. You couldn't tell whether they were sore, happy, insulted—anything. He shook his head quickly at Slimmy—the little man was pushing things a little.

However, Its Wonders didn't seem annoyed by the refusal of his word. "We could," he said, "destroy each other's weapons."

"Would you agree to such a proposition?"

"Yes," chorused the three Martians.

Once they were together again in their emasculated ship, Slimmy and Bell compared notes.

"What's their ship like?" Slimmy wanted to know.

"Smooth," said Bell. "An Ikarion 44, with all the fixin's. Got that old-style ether-cloud steering for hyper-space travel, though—you know—the one that builds etheric resistance on one bow or the other to turn the ship when she's traveling faster than light? We can outmaneuver them if it comes to a chase."

Slimmy grinned. "That bootleg ether rudder of ours is so perfect because it's so simple, but it's not the easiest thing in the world to adapt to an Ikarion. How's their spatial steering?"

"Same as ours," answered Bell. "So all we need is the process and a small start. Fat chance ... By the way—remember what Its Wonders said about the killer field's stopping a spy ray? That was a slip on his part. I got looking for one when I was busting up their big guns. They have one, sure enough—a neat, little portable, sound and viviscreen; and I'll bet my back teeth it records. We got to watch our mouths."

"Yeah." Slimmy walked over and drew himself a flask of cocola, then came and sat on his bunk next to Bell.

Bell was surprised to find that on the way Slimmy had snatched up the cellotab and stylus. He took it, shielded it closely, and began to write as he talked about the Martian ship. In a few minutes he passed the tablet to Slimmy. It read:

"A laugh for you. Heaven and Its Wonders no sooner got out of here when they began to pump me about why you'd tried to kill me just before we landed. We were right; they saw you shooting me with the water pistol and it threw their mental gears into six speeds at once. Couldn't understand why you didn't kill me or why I didn't kill you for trying. Suggested that if I wanted to slip you the double-x, they'd see to it that you were killed. Gave me a phial of Martian paralysis virus. Told me that if we found the Artnan secret, if I killed you with the virus, I'd be protected when they brought me back to the System."

"Yep," said Slimmy aloud as he reached for the stylus, "them Martians are certainly nice fellers."

Bellew motioned to Slimmy to duck the cellotab, winked, stretched and said, "You think we ought to grab some sleep?"

Slimmy said, "Why, sure," with admirable promptness, considering that both of them had had the sleepcenters removed from their brains by outlaw Earth surgeons in preparation for the trip.

While Slimmy pulled off his shoes, Bell went to a locker and slid two pairs of thick spectacles under his tunic, along with two disks of the same material as the lenses. He switched off the lights, pulled his own bunk out from the bulkhead over Slimmy's, dropped a pair of spectacles and a disk on the little man's chest, and rolled into bed. Both men clipped the disks to their bunklights, switched them on, and donned the glasses. Martians, possessing vision far into the ultraviolet, are blind to the reds merging into the infrared which is so prevalent on their own planet. If the spy ray was functioning—and of course it was—all the screen showed was a lot of nothing on a background of the same, and all the amplifier picked up was the tiny whisper of a busy stylus.

"Been thinking about those Artnans," wrote Bell. "What do you suppose is the reason for their building that transmutation shed on the surface of the planet if their civilization is underground?"

"To be near the transmitter, I'd imagine. Far as I know, a probability wave can't operate below ground."

"Seems likely. What's your guess about the process?"

"That, bud, is our little stymie. The Martians have tested the ground right clear up to the edge of the killer field for vibrations from machinery. They heard the footsteps and the burrowing of the Artnans, and the noise from the Prob.-wave transmitter and receiver. But that's all. Artnan workers—not more than eight or ten at a time—tend whatever's in that shed. Now and then a blast of artificial wind rushes through the shed. Right afterward big suction intakes gather up a powdery material and collect it in the hoppers which feed '235 into the transmitter. Then the wind blasts back with a slightly heavier powder. There's also a little vegetative sound—spores popping and whatnot but our Martian friends don't know whether there is some plant life in the shed or whether the vibrations come from the flora outside. That's a lot of info to get from ground vibrations but you know Martian detection instruments."

"Wonder what the Artnans do with the boron they get from Mars?" Slimmy wrote after a silent interval.

"Eat it, I guess. For all we know, the whole set-up that has made Earth a slave and put Mars on the economic rocks may be just a side line to the Artnans. Maybe it's candy to them, or a liquor industry. That's something we'll never know as long as the Artnans act so unsociable."

"They don't behave like an outfit that's trying to keep a monopoly," Slimmy scrawled. "Seems to me their very treatment of us and the Martians is their way of telling us, 'We found the process. If you want to dig it up for yourselves, go to it.' They don't seem to give much of a damn whether we do or not."

"Seems sound enough. I wish we could get some slant on their psychology. Their reasoning is so absolutely alien to anything we have in our System. Old Laidlaw was right."

Bell handed this to Slimmy and then snatched it back excitedly. "*The Laidlaw Hypothesis!*" he underlined. "That's the answer! Laidlaw said that each Solar System had civilizations and cultures with a common ancestor, which ancestor was peculiar to the System. For that reason there is no way of predicting in what direction a new system's fauna will evolve. The Artnans are mineral eaters, right? Then, according to Laidlaw, their plants have a corresponding metabolism, and so has every other living thing in the system! Do you see what I'm getting at?"

"No," said Slimmy aloud, forgetting himself. Bell snatched the pad and belted the little man's mouth with it before he wrote:

"It isn't an apparatus process, dope! The Artnans don't transmute '238 into '235 by electrochemistry or radiophysics or any other process we ever heard of! Those Artnans in the shed aren't scientists or even mechanics! They're *gardeners!*"

"Plants?" Slimmy's amazement dug the stylus deep into the cellotab. "How can plants transmute one isotope into another?"

"An Artnan might like to know how an Earth plant can change light and water and minerals into cellulose," wrote Bell. "Now; plant or mold or fungus—what sort of a place might it come from?"

"Not here," was Slimmy's prompt reply. "The atmosphere is slightly humid. Water and pure '235 don't mix. Any plant that gave off atomic fuel that way would blow itself from here to Scranton. It must have been brought here from an airless planet or satellite too hot or too cold for water to exist."

"Is there such a body in this system?"

In answer, Slimmy rolled out of his bunk and went to the chart desk, returning with a sketched astro map of the system.

"Two," he wrote on the edge of the chart. "This one"—an arrow indicated a large planet far away from the double sun—"and this peanut here. A ninety-six day year, son, and it's hot. I mean, but torrid. Don't tell me anything from there could live here, if at all."

"Might, if it's a mold, or a bacterium. Temperature wouldn't make much difference to a really simple metallic mold. It's worth a try. How do we get out there without taking our three little playmates with us?"

They thought that over for a while, and then Slimmy giggled and wrote, "Buddy, I feel an awful attack of Martian paralysis coming on!"

Bell snapped his fingers, lay back in his bunk and roared with laughter.

Heaven, Its Wonders and Hell squatted excitedly before the portable spy-ray set in the center of their control room, watching the scene it pictured. Slimmy's head protruded from a small iron lung built into the bulkhead, and his head was stretched back so far that the skin on his neck seemed on the breaking point. His face was bluish; there was a thin line of foam on his lips, and his breath whispered whistling through the annunciator.

"Traitorous creature," piped Its Wonders. "He has taken our advice and inoculated his companion with the disease."

Heaven waved his eye stalks. "Where is that Earthman, anyway?"

A loud *thuck! thuck!* answered his question, as Bell Bellew banged on the insulated gate to the Martians' air lock. Heaven reached out a long, jointless arm and pressed a panel; the door opened.

"Hey," Bell roared before he was well into the room, "you guys better come a-runnin'. My partner's went and got himself some Martian paralysis and he can't last much longer." Bell permitted himself a leer.

"What has that to do with us?" Heaven wanted to know.

"Everything. He has the secret of the Artnan process. His voice is gone now; all he can do is gurgle. I ain't telepathic; you are. His gurgles ought to make some sense to you."

"You stupid primitive," squeaked Its Wonders. "What do you mean by inoculating him and endangering the secret? If he dies with it, we may never discover it!"

Bell looked sheepish. "Well, it was this way," he said. "Slimmy figured it all out. Said it was simple once you got the idea—one of those things that's so evident you can't see it. I asked him what it was. He wouldn't say. Said he'd tell me if his life was in danger, but not before. It was too dangerous for both of us to know. I got to thinking. If we got back to Earth with the secret, we'd have no chance of keeping it from Mars. Mars would take the process and kill us for our pains. Why should I get myself killed? If I tied in with you, I had your promise of protection. So I slipped him the virus, thinkin' he'd tell me the process when he knew what was the matter with him. But it hit him too fast. I can't understand a word. Come on—he may be dead before we get there!" So saying, the big Earthman turned and bolted out of the Martian ship.

The Martians held a shrill consultation and then took out after Bell, their thin claws eating up the distance. Bell was running with everything he had, but the Martians passed him before he had gone an eighth of the way. They were not even breathing hard.

Martian paralysis is sure death to the people of the red planet. When Bell got to the ship he found the three Martians pressing as close to Slimmy as they dared, which was about five feet. They were straining to hear what Slimmy was mumbling, and stared annoyedly when Bell burst in.

"Get away from him," Bell wheezed. "Dammit, now you'll never get the information. He'd die before he'd tell it to a Martian."

"Be quiet!" snapped Hell. "He is past that. The paralysis strikes first at the eyes, then at the hearing. He doesn't know who is here."

Slimmy's tortured voice broke from moans into words. "Bell . . . process . . . electrolyzation of . . . dying, I guess . . . lousy Martian . . . process . . . electrolyzation of —" Suddenly he made a tremendous effort, lifted his head, and said in a perfectly normal conversational tone, "We're rick-bijitting for a dew-jaw." Then his head snapped back and he lay still.

Bell blundered over to the after bulkhead, ripped open the cold locker, and tossed three flasks of cocola to the Martians. "Drink up," he snapped. "You're going to need all your brains from now on if you're going to savvy *that*." He waved a hand toward Slimmy, who was babbling busily away about fortissing a sanzzifranz.

The Martians sucked away eagerly at the frothy liquid; willing to do anything that would sharpen their senses.

So Slimmy muttered and the Martians guzzled, and in forty minutes Bell stopped passing out cocola and went to the iron lung and opened it, and Slimmy climbed out, rubbing his neck and cussing softly.

"That was a long haul, Bell," he complained.

"You did fine, kid," said Bell. "I must remember to slip you the real thing sometime."

"What are we going to do with these disgustingly intemperate creatures?" asked Slimmy, indicating the Martians.

They were propped up against the bulkhead, limp eye stalks registering their impotent rage. They were absolutely helpless, though their implacable brains were clicking away like high-speed calculating machines.

Bell thought, and snickered: "You stick around and watch 'em. I'm going to take a ride. I'll leave fifty gallons of coke with you. They're too plastered to keep you from opening their ugly faces and pouring more coke in. Don't let them sober up. Just keep telling them that they'll drink it or you'll drown them in it."

Together they lifted the limp bodies and dropped them in the sand outside. "We ought to knock them off," said Slimmy.

"I thought of that. But if you could see farther than your excuse for a nose, you might remember that we have nothing but a shrewd guess as to the accuracy of our idea about the process. If we're wrong, these guys might come in handy again."

"Anything you say," said Slimmy reluctantly. "I'll take good care of them until you get back. After that, I can't promise. Take care of yourself, incidentally."

"Worry not, little man. Ought to be back inside of fifty hours. So long." He slapped Slimmy's back and dove back into the ship.

The port closed with a clang, and the silver ship rose, circled twice, and dwindled to a point before it slipped under the horizon. Slimmy looked after it longingly and then turned to the helpless Martians.

"Time for your bottles, babies," he said, and went to work pouring the cocola into their gullets.

Bell followed the planet's surface until he was sure he was out of sight of the drunken Martians, and then curved up and away into space. As soon as he was out of the planet's effective space warp, he slipped into hyperspace and traveled toward Procyon and its dark companion at many times the speed of light. Watching his chronometers closely, he spun dials and flipped switches in each phase of acceleration and deceleration, and then went spatial again not two thousand miles from the inner planet. In spite of the almost perfect physical insulation of the craft, it was already growing warmer in the control room. Bellew set up a small warp around the ship to convert the heat into light that could be sent back toward the twin suns, and then began circling the planet. Delicate instruments felt into the depths of every crater, every boiling sea of rock on the hot little world. Bell let the ship fall into an orbit, and with one eye glued to a teleo-spectrograph and the other to his detector instruments, he searched every inch of area as it passed beneath him. The hunt didn't take long—there was uranium aplenty down there. There were great pits of U-236 and '37, something he didn't know existed in the Universe, so rare are they.

But—and his teeth flashed in a wide grin as he saw it—there were correspondingly great masses of both '238 and '235. He brought the ship close to the surface, cloaked in its light-building warp, near a fiery plain where both isotopes could be detected. Through a screened telescope he saw what he was after—a field of writhing growth, nearly hidden by a fine dust of spores. They weren't plants—they were molds; and at enormous magnification he observed their life-cycle as they ate into the uranium, turning the rarer isotopes into their structures, throwing out all impurities, including U-235. Their rate of metabolism was astonishingly fast; and when a colony of them had exhausted all the uranium near it, the molds cast off their spores and died. The spores, heavily encysted, drifted about in the hot gases at the surface, until the nearness of their food drew them to the planet's semimolten surface. Then they sprouted, fed, spored and died again.

Bellew let his ship settle even more, and dropped a tube of berylu-steel from the hull to a drift of spores. A few of them were drawn upward by the suction he set up; then, tube and all, he snapped the ship into space. Once out there, he experimented briefly and thoroughly with his prize. The mold certainly filled the bill. The cysts apparently could stay alive without nourishment indefinitely. They germinated readily at any temperature, as long as they were in the presence of uranium. Happily, Bellew slipped into hyperspace and dove back toward Artna.

The search of the inner planet and the capture of the spores had taken considerably longer than Bell had expected; he was twenty hours overdue when at last he sighted the great Artnan probability wave transmitter. He cast about anxiously for the spot where he had left Slimmy and the Martians. There was nothing there but tumbled sand.

Bell flung the ship down and, through a telescope, examined the ground. There had been a scuffle, apparently, and if Bell knew Slimmy, it must have been a pip, in spite of the fact that Martians are three times as strong as any human.

"A hell of a mess," he murmured, and swung the ship toward the hollow where lay the Martian cruiser.

Landing next to it, he hunted through Slimmy's locker until he found what he wanted, concealed in a cleverly devised secret compartment. Then he opened the air lock and strode over to the Martian ship.

The port swung open as he approached. Its Wonders stood there, apparently suffering little from what must have been quite a hangover. "What do you want?"

"Slimmy. What have you done with him?"

"Your companion is safe. He will be returned to you alive if you give us what you went away to get."

"You've killed him!"

Its Wonders stood aside. "Come in and see for yourself."

Bell pushed past him. Slimmy was there, looking very sheepish in the iron grip of the other two Martians.

"Hiya, boy," he said.

"Slimmy! What happened?"

"What happened to you in Cincinnati that night we spent at Bert's place?"

Bellew remembered the occasion. He wasn't proud of it. He'd tried to outdrink half a dozen boron miners and had failed rather miserably. He remembered with distaste the oily feeling at the pit of his stomach, and how liquor had suddenly turned from one of the greater pleasures of life into nothing more nor less than an emetic. "What's that got to do—"

"They fooled me, that's all. After you'd been gone about eight hours or so they stopped trying not to swallow the stuff and began to get greedy. I missed the gag—I fed it to them as fast as they would take it. They all got sick. Very sick. Then they started to sober up, and I had to feed 'em more while they were still weak. Gallon for gallon, they threw off what I fed them. I don't know how they did it—they sure can take it. Anyhow, I ran plumb out of cocola. We shoulda killed 'em."

"We will," said Bell grimly, his jaw bunching. "O.K., fellers—let him go now." He reached casually into his pocket and pulled out a blue-steel automatic blaster. The Martians stiffened indignantly.

"Where did you get that?" said Heaven. "We had your promise to allow us to destroy every weapon you had aboard. You destroyed all of ours. How is it you kept that?"

Again Bell found himself wishing that a Martian could express emotion. He'd have given anything to know just how mad the tall Martian was.

"This," said Bellew, stepping aside to let the released Slimmy past him, "is what we call, on Earth, an ace in the hole."

The Martians started and stopped a concerted rush at Bell as he glanced over to see if Slimmy was safe in the silver ship, and then turned to them again.

"Nice to've known you," he said, and backed out.

As the Earth ship rose gently away from Artna, Slimmy looked happily up from the controls. "You know, Bell, in spite of the fact that it was a dirty trick to hold out that blaster after giving our word, I'm glad you did it."

Bell looked at the blaster and grinned, moving toward the refuse lock. "Swing her a little left," he said, sighting through a port. "You got the wrong idea, chum." He dropped the gun into the lock, closed the upper door, and put his hand on the dumping lever. "We promised to let them destroy all our deadly weapons. They did. Am I glad to do *this!*" and he threw the lever. The gun curved down and dropped right in front of the air lock of the Martian ship. Three lanky figures pounced on it, and a jet of soapy water shot futilely up at them.

Science-fiction sneers at science: A television "mirror," non-reversing, was a great crowd-catcher at Radio City this year (1948). Science sneers at science-fiction: Color television is already a commercial reality!

ETHER BREATHER was my first science-fiction story. It might be of interest to remark here that the scanning-disc set, mentioned here in sneering terms, was, at the time of writing, the only widely-used method of video-transmission, while the iconoscope was a laboratory locus for the wishful thinking of ambitious electronicians.

Ether Breather

It was "The Seashell." It *would* have to be "The Seashell." I wrote it first as a short story, and it was turned down. Then I made a novelette out of it, and then a novel. Then a short short. Then a three-line gag. And it still wouldn't sell. It got to be a fetish with me, rewriting that "Seashell." After a while editors got so used to it that they turned it down on sight. I had enough rejection slips from that number alone to paper every room in the house of tomorrow. So when it sold—well, it was like the death of a friend. It hit me. I hated to see it go.

It was a play by that time, but I hadn't changed it much. Still the same pastel, frou-frou old "Seashell" story, about two children who grew up and met each other only three times as the years went on, and a little seashell that changed hands each time they met. The plot, if any, doesn't matter. The dialogue was—well, pastel. Naïve. Unsophisticated. Very pretty, and practically salesproof. But it just happened to ring the bell

73

with an earnest young reader for Associated Television, Inc., who was looking for something about that length that could be dubbed "artistic"; something that would not require too much cerebration on the part of an audience, so that said audience could relax and appreciate the new polychrome technique of television transmission. You know; pastel.

As I leaned back in my old relic of an armchair that night, and watched the streamlined version of my slow-moving brainchild, I had to admire the way they put it over. In spots it was almost good, that "Seashell." Well suited for the occasion, too. It was a full-hour program given free to a perfume house by Associated, to try out the new color transmission as an advertising medium. I liked the first two acts, if I do say so as shouldn't. It was at the half-hour mark that I got my first kick on the chin. It was a two-minute skit for the advertising plug.

A tall and elegant couple were seen standing on marble steps in an elaborate theater lobby. Says she to he:

"And how do you like the play, Mr. Robinson?"

Says he to she: "It stinks."

Just like that. Like any radio-television listener, I was used to paying little, if any attention to a plug. That certainly snapped me up in my chair. After all, it was my play, even if it was "The Seashell." They couldn't do that to me.

But the girl smiling archly out of my television set didn't seem to mind. She said sweetly, "I think so, too."

He was looking slushily down into her eyes. He said: "That goes for you, too, my dear. What *is* that perfume you are using?"

"Berbelot's *Doux Rêves*. What do you think of it?"

He said, "You heard what I said about the play."

I didn't wait for the rest of the plug, the station identification, and act three. I headed for my visiphone and dialed Associated. I was burning up. When their pert-faced switchboard girl flashed on my screen I snapped: "Get me Griff. Snap it up!"

"Mr. Griff's line is busy, Mr. Hamilton," she sang to

me. "Will you hold the wire, or shall I call you back?"

"None of that, Dorothe," I roared. Dorothe and I had gone to high school together; as a matter of fact I had got her the job with Griff, who was Associated's head script man. "I don't care who's talking to Griff. Cut him off and put me through. He can't do that to me. I'll sue, that's what I'll do. I'll break the company. I'll—"

"Take it easy, Ted," she said. "What's the matter with everyone all of a sudden, anyway? If you must know, the man gabbing with Griff now is old Berbelot himself. Seems he wants to sue Associated, too. What's up?"

By this time I was practically incoherent. "Berbelot, hey? I'll sue him, too. The rat! The dirty— What are you laughing at?"

"He wants to sue you!" she giggled. "And I'll bet Griff will, too, to shut Berbelot up. You know, this might turn out to be really funny!" Before I could swallow that she switched me over to Griff.

As he answered he was wiping his heavy jowls with a handkerchief. "Well?" he asked in a shaken voice.

"What are you, a wise guy?" I bellowed. "What kind of a stunt is that you pulled on the commercial plug on my play? Whose idea was that, anway? Berbelot's? What the—"

"Now, Hamilton," Griff said easily, "don't excite yourself this way." I could see his hands trembling— evidently old Berbelot had laid it on thick. "Nothing untoward has occurred. You must be mistaken. I assure you—"

"You pompous old," I growled, waiving a swell two-dollar word on him, "don't call me a liar. I've been listening to that program and I know what I heard. I'm going to sue you. And Berbelot. And if you try to pass the buck onto the actors in that plug skit, I'll sue them, too. And if you make any more cracks about me being mistaken, I'm going to come up there and feed you your teeth. Then I'll sue you personally as well as Associated."

I dialed out and went back to my television set, fuming. The program was going on as if nothing had happened. As I cooled—and I cool slowly—I began to see that the last half of "The Seashell" was even better than the first. You know, it's poison for a writer to fall in love with his own stuff; but, by golly, sometimes you turn out a piece that really has something. You try to be critical, and you can't be. The Ponta Delgada sequence in "The Seashell" was like that.

The girl was on a cruise and the boy was on a training ship. They met in the Azores Islands. Very touching. The last time they saw each other was before they were in their teens, but in the meantime they had had their dreams. Get the idea of the thing? Very pastel. And they did do it nicely. The shots of Ponta Delgada and the scenery of the Azores were swell. Came the moment, after four minutes of icky dialogue, when he gazed at her, the light of true, mature love dawning on his young face.

She said shyly, "Well—"

Now, his lines, as written—and I should know!—went:

"Rosalind ... it *is* you, then, isn't it? Oh, I'm afraid"—he grasps her shoulders—"afraid that it can't be real. So many times I've seen someone who might be you, and it has never been ... Rosalind, Rosalind, guardian angel, reason for living, beloved . . . beloved—" Clinch.

Now, as I say, it went off as written, up to and including the clinch. But then came the payoff. He took his lips from hers, buried his face in her hair and said clearly: "I hate your ——— guts." And that "———" was the most perfectly enunciated present participle of a four-letter verb I have ever heard.

Just what happened after that I couldn't tell you. I went haywire, I guess. I scattered two hundred and twenty dollars' worth of television set over all three rooms of my apartment. Next thing I knew I was in a 'press tube, hurtling toward the three-hundred-story skyscraper that housed Associated Television. Never have I seen one of those 'press cars, forced by compressed air through tubes under the city, move so slowly, but it might have been my imagination. If I had anything to do with it, there was going to be one dead script boss up there.

And whom should I run into on the 229th floor but old Berbelot himself? The perfume king had blood in his eye. Through the haze of anger that surrounded me, I began to realize that things were about to be very tough on Griff. And I was quite ready to help out all I could.

Berbelot saw me at the same instant, and seemed to read my thought. "Come on," he said briefly, and together we ran the gantlet of secretaries and assistants and burst into Griff's office.

Griff rose to his feet and tried to look dignified, with little success. I leaped over his glass desk and pulled the wings of his stylish open-necked collar together until he began squeaking.

Berbelot seemed to be enjoying it. "Don't kill him, Hamilton," he said after a bit. "I want to."

I let the script man go. He sank down to the floor, gasping. He was like a scared kid, in more ways than one. It was funny.

We let him get his breath. He climbed to his feet, sat down at his desk, and reached out toward a battery of push buttons. Berbelot snatched up a Dow-metal knife and hacked viciously at the chubby hand. It retreated.

"Might I ask," said Griff heavily, "the reason for this unprovoked rowdiness?"

Berbelot cocked an eye at me. "Might he?"

"He might tell us what this monkey business is all about," I said.

Griff cleared his throat painfully. "I told both you ... er ... gentlemen over the phone that, as far as I know, there was nothing amiss in our interpretation of your play, Mr. Hamilton, nor in the commercial section of the broadcast, Mr. Berbelot. After your protests over the wire, I made it a point to see the second half of the broadcast myself. Nothing was wrong. And as this is the first commercial color broadcast, it has been recorded. If you are not satisfied with my statements, you are welcome to see the recording yourselves, immediately."

What else could we want? It occurred to both of us that Griff was really up a tree; that he was telling the truth as far as he knew it, and that he thought we were both screwy. I began to think so myself.

Berbelot said, "Griff, didn't you hear that dialogue near the end, when those two kids were by the sea wall?"

Griff nodded.

"Think back now," Berbelot went on. "What did the boy say to the girl when he put his muzzle into her hair?"

"'I love you,'" said Griff self-consciously, and blushed. "He said it twice."

Berbelot and I looked at each other. "Let's see that recording," I said.

Well, we did, in Griff's luxurious private projection room. I hope I never have to live through an hour like that again. If it weren't for the fact that Berbelot was seeing the same thing I saw, and feeling the same way about it, I'd have reported to an alienist. Because that program came off Griff's projector positively shimmering with innocuousness. My script was A-1; Berbelot's plugs were right. On that plug that had started everything, where the man and the girl were gabbing in the theater lobby, the dialogue went like this:

"And how do you like the play, Mr. Robinson?"

"Utterly charming . . . and that goes for you, too, my dear. What *is* that perfume you are using?"

"Berbelot's *Doux Rêves*. What do you think of it?"

"You heard what I said about the play,"

Well there you are. And, by the recording, Griff had been right about the repetitious three little words in the Azores sequence. I was floored.

After it was over, Berbelot said to Griff: "I think I can speak for Mr. Hamilton when I say that if this is an actual recording, we owe you an apology; also when I say that we do not accept your evidence until we have compiled our own. I recorded that program as it came over my set, as I have recorded all my advertising. We will see you tomorrow, and we will bring that sound film. Coming, Hamilton?"

I nodded and we left, leaving Griff to chew his lip.

I'd like to skip briefly over the last chapter of that evening's nightmare. Berbelot picked up a camera expert on the way, and we had the films developed within an hour after we arrived at the fantastic "house that perfume built." And if I was crazy, so was Berbelot; and if he was, then so was the camera. So help me, that blasted program came out on Berbelot's screen exactly as it had on my set and his. If anyone ever took a long-distance cussing-out, it was Griff that night. We figured, of course, that he had planted a phony recording on us, so that we wouldn't sue. He'd do the same thing in court, too. I told Berbelot so. He shook his head.

"No, Hamilton, we can't take it to court. Associated gave me that broadcast, the first color commercial, on condition that I sign away their responsibility for 'incomplete, or inadequate, or otherwise unsatisfactory performance.' They didn't quite trust that new apparatus, you know."

"Well, I'll sue for both of us, then," I said.

"Did they buy all rights?" he asked.

"Yes . . . damn! They got me, too! They have a legal right to do anything they want." I threw my cigarette into the electric fire and snapped on Berbelot's big television set, tuning it to Associated's XZB.

Nothing happened.

"Hey! Your set's on the bum!" I said. Berbelot got up and began fiddling with the dial. I was wrong. There was nothing the matter with the set. It was Associated. All of their stations were off the air—all four of them. We looked at each other.

"Get XZW," said Berbelot. "It's an Associated affiliate, under cover. Maybe we can—"

XZW blared out at us as I spun the dial. A dance program, the new five-beat stuff. Suddenly the announcer stuck his face into the transmitter.

"A bulletin from Iconoscope News Service," he said conversationally. "FCC has clamped down on Associated Television and its stations. They are off the air. The reasons were not given, but it is surmised that it has to do with a little strong language used on the world première of Associated's new color transmission. That is all."

"I expected that," smiled Berbelot. "Wonder how Griff'll alibi himself out of that? If he tries to use that recording of his, I'll most cheerfully turn mine over to the government, and we'll have him for perjury."

"Sorta tough on Associated, isn't it?" I said.

"Not particularly. You know these big corporations. Associated gets millions out of their four networks, but those millions are just a drop in the bucket compared with the other pies they've got their fingers in. That color technique, for instance. Now that they can't use it for a while, how many other outfits will miss the chance of bidding for the method and equipment? They lose some advertising contracts, and they save by not operating. They won't even feel it. I'll bet you'll see color transmission within forty-eight hours over a rival network."

He was right. Two days later Cineradio had a color broadcast scheduled, and all hell broke loose. What they'd done to the Berbelot hour and my "Seashell" was really tame.

The program was sponsored by one of the antigravity industries—I forget which. They'd hired Raouls Stavisk, the composer, to play one of the ancient Gallic operas he'd exhumed. It was a piece called "Carmen" and had been practically forgotten for two centuries. News of it had created quite a stir among music lovers, although, personally, I don't go for it. It's too barbaric for me. Too hard to listen to, when you've been hearing five-beat all your life. And those old-timers had never heard of a quarter tone.

Anyway, it was a big affair, televised right from the huge Citizens' Auditorium. It was more than half full —there were about 130,000 people there. Practically all of the select highbrow music fans from that section of the city. Yes, 130,000 pairs of eyes saw that show in the flesh, and countless millions saw it on their own sets; remember that.

Those that saw it at the Auditorium got their money's worth, from what I hear. They saw the complete opera; saw it go off as scheduled. The coloratura, Maria Jeff, was in perfect voice, and Stavisk's orchestra rendered the ancient tones perfectly. So what?

So, those that saw it at home saw the first half of the program the same as broadcast—of course. But—and get this—they saw Maria Jeff, on a close-up, in the middle of an aria, throw back her head, stop singing, and shout raucously: "The hell with this! Whip it up, boys!"

They heard the orchestra break out of the old two-four music—"Habañera," I think they called it—and slide into a wicked old-time five-beat song about "alco-pill Alice," the girl who didn't believe in eugenics. They saw her step lightly about the stage, shedding her costume—not that I blame her for that; it was supposed to be authentic, and must have been warm. But there was a certain something about the way she did it.

I've never seen or heard of anything like it. First, I thought that it was part of the opera, because from what I learned in school I gather that the ancient people used to go in for things like that. I wouldn't know. But I knew it wasn't opera when old Stavisk himself jumped up on the stage and started dancing with the prima donna. The televisors flashed around the audience, and there they were, every one of them, dancing in the aisles. And I mean dancing. Wow!

Well, you can imagine the trouble that that caused. Cineradio, Inc., was flabbergasted when they were shut down by FCC like Associated. So were 130,000 people who had seen the opera and thought it was good. Every last one of them denied dancing in the aisles. No one had seen Stavisk jump on the stage. It just didn't make sense.

Cineradio, of course, had a recording. So, it turned out, did FCC. Each recording proved the point of its respective group. That of Cineradio, taken by a sound camera right there in the auditorium, showed a musical program. FCC's, photographed right off a government standard receiver, showed the riot that I and millions of others had seen over the air. It was too much for me. I went out to see Berbelot. The old boy had a lot of sense, and he'd seen the beginning of the crazy business.

He looked pleased when I saw his face on his house televisor. "Hamilton!" he exclaimed. "Come on in! I've been phoning all over the five downtown boroughs for you!" He pressed a button and the foyer door behind me closed. I was whisked up into his rooms. That combination foyer and elevator of his is a nice gadget.

"I guess I don't have to ask you why you came," he said as we shook hands. "Cineradio certainly pulled a boner, hey?"

"Yes and no," I said. "I'm beginning to think that Griff was right when he said that, as far as he knew, the program was on the up and up. But if he was right, what's it all about? How can a program reach the transmitters in perfect shape, and come out of every receiver in the nation like a practical joker's idea of paradise?"

"It can't," said Berbelot. He stroked his chin thoughtfully. "But it did. Three times."

"Three—When—"

"Just now, before you got in. The secretary of state was making a speech over XZM, Consolidated Atomic, you know. XZM grabbed the color equipment from Cineradio as soon as they were blacked out by FCC. Well, the honorable secretary droned on as usual for just twelve and a half minutes. Suddenly he stopped, grinned into the transmitter, and said, "Say, have you heard the one about the traveling farmer and the salesman's daughter?"

"I have," I said. "My gosh, don't tell me he spieled it?"

"Right," said Berbelot. "In detail, over the unsullied airwaves. I called up right away, but couldn't get through. XZM's trunk lines were jammed. A very worried-looking switchboard girl hooked up I don't know how many lines together and anounced into them: "If you people are calling up about the secretary's speech, there is nothing wrong with it. Now please get off the lines!' "

"Well," I said, "let's see what we've got. First, the broadcasts leave the studios as scheduled and as written. Shall we accept that?"

"Yes," said Berbelot. "Then, since so far no black-and-white broadcasts have been affected, we'll consider that this strange behavior is limited to the polychrome technique."

"How about the recordings at the studios? They were in polychrome, and they weren't affected."

Berbelot pressed a button, and an automatic serving table rolled out of its niche and stopped in front of each of us. We helped ourselves to smokes and drinks, and the table returned to its place.

"Cineradio's wasn't a television recording, Hamilton. It was a sound camera. As for Associated's ... I've got it! Griff's recording was transmitted to his recording machines by wire, from the studios! It didn't go out on the air at all!"

"You're right. Then we can assume that the only programs affected are those in polychrome, actually aired. Fine, but where does that get us?"

"Nowhere," admitted Berbelot. "But maybe we can find out. Come with me."

We stepped into an elevator and dropped three floors. "I don't know if you've heard that I'm a television bug," said my host. "Here's my lab. I flatter myself that a more complete one does not exist anywhere."

I wouldn't doubt it. I never in my life saw a layout like that. It was part museum and part workshop. It had in it a copy or a genuine relic of each and every phase of television down through the years, right from the old original scanning-disk sets to the latest three-dimensional atomic jobs. Over in the corner was an extraordinarily complicated mass of apparatus which I recognized as a polychrome transmitter.

"Nice job, isn't it?" said Berbelot. "It was developed in here, you know, by one of the lads who won the Berbelot scholarship." I hadn't known. I began to have real respect for this astonishing man.

"Just how does it work?" I asked him.

"Hamilton," he said testily, "we have work to do. I would be talking all night if I told you. But the general idea is that the vibrations sent out by this transmitter are all out of phase with each other. Tinting in the receiver is achieved by certain blendings of these out-of-phase vibrations as they leave this rig. The effect is a sort of irregular vibration—a vibration in the electromagnetic waves themselves, resulting in a totally new type of wave which is still receivable in a standard set."

"I see," I lied. "Well, what do you plan to do?"

"I'm going to broadcast from here to my country place up north. It's eight hundred miles away from here, which ought to be sufficient. My signals will be received there and automatically returned to us by wire." He indicated a receiver standing close by. "If there is any difference between what we send and what we get, we can possibly find out just what the trouble is."

"How about FCC?" I asked. "Suppose—it sounds funny to say it—but just suppose that we get the kind of strong talk that came over the air during my 'Seashell' number?"

Berbelot snorted. "That's taken care of. The broadcast will be directional. No receiver can get it but mine."

What a man! He thought of everything. "O.K.," I said. "Let's go."

Berbelot threw a couple of master switches and we sat down in front of the receiver. Lights blazed on, and through a bank of push buttons at his elbow, Berbelot maneuvered the transmitting cells to a point above and behind the receiver, so that we could see and be seen without turning our heads. At a nod from Berbelot I leaned forward and switched on the receiver.

Berbelot glanced at his watch. "If things work out right, it will be between ten and thirty minutes before we get any interference." His voice sounded a little metallic. I realized that it was coming from the receiver as he spoke.

The images cleared on the view-screen as the set warmed up. It gave me an odd sensation. I saw Berbelot and myself sitting side by side—just as if we were sitting in front of a mirror, except that the images were not reversed. I thumbed my nose at myself, and my image returned the compliment.

Berbelot said: "Go easy, boy. If we get the same kind of interference the others got, your image will make something out of that." He chuckled.

"Damn right," said the receiver.

Berbelot and I stared at each other, and back at the screen. Berbelot's face was the same, but mine had a vicious sneer on it. Berbelot calmly checked with his watch. "Eight forty-six," he said. "Less time each broadcast. Pretty soon the interference will start with the broadcast, if this keeps up."

"Not unless you start broadcasting on a regular schedule," said Berbelot's image.

It had apparently dissociated itself completely from Berbelot himself. I was floored.

Berbelot sat beside me, his face frozen. "You see?" he whispered to me. "It takes a minute to catch up with itself. Till it does, it is my image."

"What does it all mean?" I gasped.

"Search me," said the perfume king.

We sat and watched. And so help me, so did our images. They were watching *us!*

Berbelot tried a direct question. "Who are you?" he asked.

"Who do we look like?" said my image; and both laughed uproariously.

Berbelot's image nudged mine. "We've got 'em on the run, hey, pal?" it chortled.

"Stop your nonsense!" said Berbelot sharply. Surprisingly, the merriment died.

"Aw," said my image plaintively. "We don't mean anything by it. Don't get sore. Let's all have fun. *I'm* having fun."

"Why, they're like kids!" I said.

"I think you're right," said Berbelot.

"Look," he said to the images, which sat there expectantly, pouting. "Before we have any fun, I want you to tell me who you are, and how you are coming through the receiver, and how you messed up the three broadcasts before this."

"Did we do wrong?" asked my image innocently. The other one giggled.

"High-spirited sons o' guns, aren't they?" said Berbelot.

"Well, are you going to answer my questions *or do I turn the transmitter off?*" he asked the images.

They chorused frantically: "We'll tell! We'll tell! Please don't turn it off!"

"What made you think of that?" I whispered to Berbelot.

"A stab in the dark," he returned. "Evidently they like coming through like this and can't do it any other way but on the polychrome wave."

"What do you want to know?" asked Berbelot's image, its lip quivering.

"Who are you?"

"Us? We're ... I don't know. You don't have a name for us, so how can I tell you?"

"Where are you?"

"Oh, everywhere. We get around."

Berbelot moved his hand impatiently toward the switch.

The images squealed: "Don't! Oh, please don't! This is fun!"

"Fun, is it?" I growled. "Come on, give us the story, or we'll black you out!"

My image said pleadingly: "Please believe us. It's the truth. We're everywhere."

"What do you look like?" I asked. "Show yourselves as you are!"

"We can't," said the other image, "because we don't 'look' like anything. We just . . . are, that's all."

"We don't reflect light," supplemented my image.

Berbelot and I exchanged a puzzled glance. Berbelot said, "Either somebody is taking us for a ride or we've stumbled on something utterly new and unheard-of."

"You certainly have," said Berbelot's image earnestly. "We've known about you for a long time—as you count time—"

"Yes," the other continued. "We knew about you some two hundred of your years ago. We had felt your vibrations for a long time before that, but we never knew just who you were until then."

"Two hundred years—" mused Berbelot. "That was about the time of the first atomic-powered television sets."

"That's right!" said my image eagerly. "It touched our brain currents and we could see and hear. We never could get through to you until recently, though, when you sent us that stupid thing about a seashell."

"None of that, now," I said angrily, while Berbelot chuckled.

"How many of you are there?" he asked them.

"One, and many. We are finite and infinite. We have no size or shape as you know it. We just . . . are."

We just swallowed that without comment. It was a bit big.

How did you change the programs? How are you changing this one?" Berbelot asked.

"These broadcasts pass directly through our brain currents. Our thoughts change them as they pass. It was impossible before; we were aware, but we could not be heard. The new wave has let us be heard. Its convolutions are in phase with our being."

"How did you happen to pick that particular way of breaking through?" I asked. "I mean all that wisecracking business."

For the first time one of the images—Berbelot's—looked abashed. "We wanted to be liked. We wanted to come through to you and find you laughing. We knew how. Two hundred years of listening to every single broadcast, public and private, has taught us your language and your emotions and your ways of thought. Did we really do wrong?"

"Looks as if we have walked into a cosmic sense of humor," remarked Berelot to me.

To his image: "Yes, in a way, you did. You lost three huge companies their broadcasting licenses. You embarrassed exceedingly a man named Griff and a secretary of state. You"——he chuckled——"made my friend here very, very angry. That wasn't quite the right thing to do, was it?"

"No," said my image. It actually blushed. "We won't do it any more. We were wrong. We are sorry."

"Aw, skip it," I said. I was embarrassed myself. "Everybody makes mistakes."

"That *is* good of you," said my image on the television screen. "We'd like to do something for you. And you, too, Mr.—"

"Berbelot," said Berbelot. Imagine introducing yourself to a television set!

"You can't do anything for us," I said, "except to stop messing up color televising."

"You really want us to stop, then?" My image turned to Berbelot's. "We have done wrong. We have hurt their feelings and made them angry."

To us: "We will not bother you again. Good-by!"

"Wait a minute!" I yelped, but I was too late. The viewscreen showed the same two figures, but they had lost their peculiar life. They were Berbelot and me. Period.

"Now look what you've done," snapped Berbelot.

He began droning into the transmitter: "Calling interrupter on polychrome wave! Can you hear me? Can you hear me? Calling—"

He broke and looked at me disgustedly. "You dope," he said quietly, and I felt like going off into a corner and bursting into tears.

Well, that's all. The FCC trials reached a "person or persons unknown" verdict, and color broadcasting became a universal reality. The world has never learned, until now, the real story of that screwy business. Berbelot spent every night for three months trying to contact that ether-intelligence, without success. Can you beat it? It waited two hundred years for a chance to come through to us, and then got its feelings hurt and withdrew!

My fault, of course. That admission doesn't help any. I wish I could do something . . .

And now . . .

Butyl and the Breather

I was still melancholic about chasing the Ether Breather out of the ken of man, the day I got that bright idea of bringing the Breather back. I should have let it stay in idea form. I should not have gone to see Berbelot about it. I also should have stayed in bed. I've got brains, but no sense. I went to see Berbelot.

He wasn't glad to see me, which he did through the televisor in his foyer. Quite a gadget, that foyer. I knew that it was an elevator to take guests up to his quarters in the mansion, the "House that Perfume Built." I hadn't known till now that it was also a highly efficient bouncing mechanism. I had no sooner passed my hand over the sensitized plate that served as a doorbell when his face appeared on the screen. He said "Hmph! Hamilton!" and next thing I knew the foyer's walls had extended and pinned me tight. I was turned upside down, shaken twice, and then dropped on my ear outside the house. I think he designed that bouncer just for me. He was a nice old boy, but, man, how he could hang on to a grouch. A whole year, this one had lasted. Just because I had been tactless with the Breather.

I got up and dusted myself off and swore I'd never bother the irascible old heel again. And then I hunted a drugstore to call him up. That's the way it was. Berbelot was a peculiar duck. His respect for me meant more than anger against him could make up for. He was the only man I ever met that ever made me sorry for anything.

I went into the visiphone booth and pressed my identification tab against the resilient panel on the phone. That made a record of the call so I could be billed for it. Then I dialed Berbelot. I got his bun-faced valet.

"I want to speak to Mr. Berbelot, Cogan."

"Mr. Berbelot is out, Mr. Hamilton."

"So!" I snapped, my voice rising. "You're the one who tossed me out just now with that salesman mangler on your doorstep! I'll macerate you, you subatomic idiot!"

"Oh . . . I . . . I didn't, Mr. Hamilton, really. I—"

"Then if you didn't Berbelot did. If he did, he's home. Incidentally, I saw him in the viewplate. Enough of the chit-chat, doughface. Tell him I want to speak to him."

"B-but he won't speak to you, Mr. Hamilton. He gave strict orders a year ago."

"Tell him I've thought of a way to get in touch with the Ether Breather again. Go on. He won't fire you, you crumb from the breadline. He'll kiss you on both cheeks. Snap into it!"

The screen went vacant as he moved away, and I heard Berbelot's voice—"I thought I told you"—and then the bumble of Cogan's, and then "WHAT!" from the old man, and another short bumble that was interrupted by Berbelot's sliding to a stop in front of the transmitter. "Hamilton," he said sternly into the visiplate, "if this is a joke of yours . . . if you think you can worm your way into my confidence with . . . if you dare to lead me on some wild-goose cha . . . if you—"

"If you'll give me a chance, King of Stink," I said, knowing that if I got him really mad he'd listen to me, being the type that got speechless with rage, "I'll give you the dope. I have an idea that I think will bring the Breather back, but it's up to you to carry it out. You have the apparatus."

"Come up," he whispered, his wattles quivering. "But I warn you, if you dare to take this liberty on a bluff, I shall most certainly have you pried loose from your esophagus."

"Comin' up!" I said. "By the way, when I get into that foyer again, please be sure which button you push."

"Don't worry," he growled, "I have a dingus up here that is quite as efficient. It throws people from the sixtieth floor. Do come up." The screen darkened. I sighed and started for the "House that Perfume Built."

The elevator glided to a stop that made my stomach feel puffy, and I stepped out. Berbelot was standing in front of it looking as suspicious as a pawnbroker. I held out my hand with some remark about how swell it was to see him again, and he just stared at it. When I thought he was going to forego the honor of shaking it, he put his hand into mine, withdrew it quickly, looked at it, and wiped it carefully on his jacket. Without his saying a word I gathered that he wasn't glad to see me, that he thought I was an undesirable and unsanitary character, and that he didn't trust me.

"Did I ever tell you," I said as calmly as I could, "that I am terribly sorry about what happened?"

Berbelot said, "I knew a man who said that after he murdered somebody. They burned him anyway."

I thought that was very nice. "Do you want to find

out about my idea or not?" I gritted. "I don't have to stay here to be insulted."

"I realize that. You're insulted everywhere, I imagine. Well, what's your idea?"

I saw Cogan hovering over the old man's shoulder and threw my hat at him. Since Berbelot apparently found it difficult to be hospitable, I saved him the trouble of inviting me to sit down by sitting down.

"Berbelot," I said, when I had one of his best cigarettes fuming as nicely as he was, "you're being unreasonable. But I have you interested, and as long as that lasts you'll be sociable. Sit down. I am about to be Socratic. It may take a little while."

"I suffer." He sat down. "I suffer exceedingly." He paused, and then added pensively, "I never thought I could be so irritated by anyone who bored me. Go ahead, Hamilton."

I closed my eyes and counted ten. Berbelot could manufacture more printable invective than anyone I ever met.

"Question one," I said. "What is the nature of the creature you dubbed Ether Breather?"

"Why, it's a . . . well, apparently a combination of etheric forces, living in and around us. It's as if the air in this room were a thinking animal. What are you—"

"I'll ask questions. Now, will you grant it intelligence?"

"Of course. A peculiar kind, though. It seems to be motivated by a childish desire to have fun—mostly at some poor human's expense."

"But its reactions were reasonable, weren't they?"

"Yes, although exaggerated. It reached us through color television; that was its only medium of expression. And it raised particular hell with the programs—a cosmic practical joker, quite uninhibited, altogether unafraid of any consequences to itself. And then when you, you blockhead, told it that it hurt someone's feelings and that it ought to get off the air, it apologized and was never heard from again. Again an exaggerated reaction. But what has that got to do with—"

"Everything. Look; you made it laugh easily. You made it ashamed of itself easily. It cried easily. If you really want to get in touch with it again, you just have to go on from there."

Berbelot pressed a concealed button and the lights took on a greenish cast. He always claimed a man thought more clearly under a green light. "I'll admit that that particular thought sequence has escaped me," he nodded, "since I do not have a mind which is led astray by illogical obscurities. But in all justice to you—not that you deserve anything approaching a compliment—I think you have something there. I suppose that is as far as you have gone, though. I've spent hours on the problem. I've called that creature for days on end on a directional polychrome wave. I've apologized to it and pleaded with it and begged it and told it funny stories and practically asked it to put its invisible feet out of my television receiver so I could kiss them. And never a whisper have I had. No, Hamilton; the Ether Breather is definitely miffed, peeved, and not at home. And it's all your fault."

"Once," I said dreamily, "I knew a woman whose husband went astray. She knew where he was, and sent him message after message. She begged and she pleaded and she wept into visiphones. It didn't get her anywhere. Then she got a bright idea. She sent him a tele-facsimile letter, written on her very best stationery. It described in great detail the nineteen different kinds of heel she thought he was."

"I don't know what this has to do with the Breather, but what happened?" asked Berbelot.

"Why, he got sore. He got so sore he dropped everything and ran home to take a poke at her!"

"Ah," said Berbelot. "And the Breather laughs easily, and you think it would—"

"It would," I nodded, "get angry easily, if we could find the right way to do it."

Berbelot rubbed his long hands together and beamed. "You're a hot-headed fool, Hamilton, and I'm convinced that your genius is a happy accident quite unattached to your hypothetical mind. But I must congratulate you for the idea. In other words, you think if we get the Breather sore enough, it will try to get even, and contact us some way or other? I'll be darned!"

"Thought you'd like it," I said.

"Well, come on," he said testily. "What are we waiting for? Let's go down to the laboratory!" Suddenly he stopped. "Er . . . Hamilton . . . this story of yours. Did that man poke his wife after he got home?"

"I dunno," I said blankly. "I just made up the story to illustrate my point. Could be."

"Hm-m-m. If the Breather decided to . . . I mean, it's a big creature, you know, and we have no idea—"

"Oh, never mind that," I laughed, "the Breather can't get past a television screen!"

Which only goes to show you how little I knew about the Ether Breather.

I was amazed by Berbelot's laboratory museum. Did you know that in the old days more than two hundred years ago, they used electrically powered sets with a ground glass, fluorescent screen built right into the end of huge cathode tubes? Imagine. And before that, they used a revolving disk with holes punctured spirally, as a scanning mechanism! They had the beginnings of frequency modulation, though. But their sets were so crude, incredible as it may seem, that atmospheric disturbances caused interference in reception! Berbelot had copies of all these old and laughable attempts at broadcasting and receiving devices.

"All right, all right," he snapped, elbow-deep in one of the first polychrome transmitters, "you've been here before. Come over here and give me a hand. You're gawking like a castor bean farmer."

I went over and followed his directions as he spot-welded, relayed, and wound a coil or two of hair-fine wire. "My gosh," I marveled, "how did you ever learn so much about television, Berbelot? I imagine it must have used up a little of your spare time to make a fortune in the perfume business."

He laughed. "I'll tell you, Hamilton," he said. "Television and perfumery are very much alike. You know yourself that no such lovely women ever walk the Earth as you see every day in the news broadcasts. For the last eighty years, since the Duval shade selector was introduced, television has given flawless complexions to all the ladies that come over the air, and bull-shoulders to all the men. It's all very phony, but it's nice to look at. Perfumery is the same proposition. A woman who smelled like a rose petal naturally would undoubtedly have something the matter with her. But science gets to work on what has been termed, through the ages, as 'B.O.' My interest in esthetically deluding the masses led me to both sciences."

"Very ingenious," I said, "but it isn't going to help you to make the Breather sore."

"My dear boy," he said, "don't be obtuse. Oh, turn down the nitrogen jets a trifle—that's it." He skillfully spotted seven leads into the video-circuit of the polychrome wave generator. "You see," he went on, running the leads over to a box control with five push buttons and a rheostat set into it, "the Breather requires very special handling. It knows us and how our minds work, or it could never have thought, for instance, of having our secretary of state recite risqué verse over the air, the first time that official used color television. Now, you are noteworthy for your spontaneity. How would you go about angering this puff of etheric wind?"

"Well, I'd . . . I'd tell it it was a dirty so-and-so. I'd insult it. I'd say it was a sissy and dare it to fight. I . . . I'd—"

"That's what I thought," said Berbelot unkindly. "You'd cuss it out in your own foul idiom, forgetting that it has no pride to take down, and as far as we know, no colleagues, communities, enamoratae, or fellows to gossip to. No, Hamilton, we can't insult it. It can insult us because it knows what we are and how we think, but we know nothing of it."

"How else can you get a being sore, then, when you

can't hold it up to ridicule or censure before itself or its fellow creatures?"

"By doing something to it personally that it won't like."

"Yeah—take a poke at it. Kick it in its vibrations. Stick a knife into its multiple personality."

Berbelot laughed. "To change the subject, for no apparent reason," he said, "have you ever run across my *Vierge Folle?*"

"A new perfume? Why, no."

Berbelot crossed the room and came back with a handful of tiny vials. "Here."

I sniffed. It was a marvelously delicate scent. It was subtle, smooth, calling up a mental picture of the veins in fine ivory. "Mmm. Nice."

"Try this one," he said. I did. It was fainter than the other; I had to draw in a lot of it before I detected the sweet, faint odor. "It's called *Casuiste,*" said Berbelot. "Now try this one. It's much fainter, you'll have to really stretch to get it at all."

"Nice business," I grinned. "Making the poor unsuspecting male get inside the circle of the vixen's arms before he's under her spell." I'd been reading some of his ad proofs. He chuckled. "That's about the idea. Here."

Berbelot handed me the vial and I expelled all the air in my lungs, hung my nose over the lip of the tube and let the air in with a roar. Next thing I knew I was strangling, staggering, swearing and letting go murderous rights and lefts at empty air. I thought I was going to die and I wished I could. When I blinked the tears out of my eyes, Berbelot was nowhere to be seen. I raged around the laboratory and finally saw him whisk around behind a massive old photoelectric transmitter. With a shriek I rushed him. He got practically inside the machine and I began taking it apart, with the firm conviction that I would keep on taking things apart long after I reached him. Luckily for him there were four thick busbars between us. He crouched behind them giggling until I reached a red-eyed state of wheezing impotence.

"Come out!" I gasped. "You ape-faced arthritic, come out of there and I'll hit you so hard you'll throttle on your shoelaces!"

"That," he said instructively, "was a quadruple quintessence of musk." He grinned. "Skunk." He looked at me and laughed outright. "Super-skunk."

I wrenched ineffectually at the bars. "A poor thing, but your very own, I'll bet," I said. "I am going to stick your arm so far down your neck you'll digest your fingernails."

"Mad, aren't you?"

"Huh?"

"I said, you're sore. I didn't cuss you out, or hold you up to ridicule, or anything, and look how mad you are!"

I began to see the light. Make the Breather angry by—"What are you gibbering about?"

He took out a white handkerchief and waved it as he unwrapped his own body from the viscera of the old-fashioned transmitter. I had to grin. What can you do with a man like that?

"O.K.," I said. "Peace, brother. But I'd suggest you treat the Breather better than you just treated me. And how in blazes you expect to get a smell like that through a polychrome transmitter is a little beyond me."

"It isn't simple," he said, "but I think it can be done. Do you know anything about the wave theory of perception?"

"Not a helluva lot," I said. "Something about a sort of spectrum arrangement of the vibrations of sensory perception, isn't it?"

"Mmm ... yes. Thought waves are of high-frequency, and although ether-borne, not of an electro-magnetic character. So also are the allied vibrations, taste and smell. Sound, too."

"Wait a minute! Sound is a purely physical vibration of air particles against our auditory apparatus."

"Of course—from the source of the sound *to* that apparatus. But from the inner ear to the hearing center in the brain, it is translated into a wave of the spectrum group I'm talking about. So with touch and sight."

"I begin to see what you're driving at. But how can you reach the Breather with these waves—providing you can produce and transmit them?"

"Oh, I can do that. Simply a matter of stepping up high-frequency emanations."

"You seem pretty confident that the Breather will be affected by the same waves that influence our senses."

"I wouldn't use the same waves. That's why I brought up the spectrum theory. Now look; we'll take thought waves of the purely internal psyche . . . the messages that relay brain impulses to different brain centers. Pure thought, with no action; pure imagery. These are of a certain wave length. We'll call it 1000. Now, take the frequencies of smell, touch and sight waves. They're 780, 850, and 960 respectively. Now, how did we contact the Ether Breather?"

"By the polychrome wave."

"That's right."

"And you mean that the ratio—"

Berbelot nodded. "The ratio between the Breather's thought waves and its sensory vibrations must be the same as that between ours."

"Why must it be?"

"Because its mental reactions are the same, as I told you before—only exaggerated. It reasons as we do, more or less. Its mental set-up corresponds with ours."

"Doggone," I said admiringly, "it's all so simple when you're told how to do it. You mean, then, to discover the ratio between what is to me a pain in the neck, and what it would be to the Breather."

"That's it. But it won't be a pain in the neck."

"Where will it be, then?"

"You're tuning in the wrong frequency," he chuckled. "I'm going to make him suffer the best way I know how, and—my business is perfumery."

"Ah," I breathed.

"Now, I'm going to cook up something really pretty. I'm going to turn out a stench that will make the Breather's illimitable edges curl!"

"From the smell of the essence of ancient egg you just gassed me with," I said, "it ought to be pretty."

"It will be. Let's see; for a base we'll use butyl mercaptan. Something sweet, and something sour—"

"—something borrowed and something blue."

"Don't be a silly romanticist." He was busy at his chemical bench. "I'll scorch a little pork fat and . . . ah. Attar of roses."

For a moment he was quiet, carefully measuring drops of liquid into a sealed exciter. Then he flipped the switch and came over to me. "It'll be ready in a jiffy. Let's rig up the transmitter."

We did as we had done before, a year ago. We maneuvered the transmitting cells of the polychrome transmitter over and above a receiver. It would send to Berbelot's country place eight hundred miles away by a directional beam, and return the signal by wire. If the Breather interfered, it would show up on the receiver. When we had done it before, we had had the odd experience of holding a conversation with our own images on the screen.

"Now I'll distill my *odeur d'ordure*," he said, "and when it's run through, you can be my guinea pig."

"Not on your life, Berbelot," I said, backing away. He grinned and went about fixing his still. It was a beautiful little glass affair, and he worked entirely under a huge bell jar in transferring it from the exciter. Butyl and burned meat and attar of roses. My gosh.

In half an hour it was ready—a dusty-brown colloid, just a few drops in the retort. "Come on, Hamilton," said Berbelot, "just a little sniff. I want to give you a preview."

"Uh-uh!" I snorted. "Here—wait."

I gave a buzz on the buzzer, and in a couple of seconds Cogan, Berbelot's valet, popped in. Cogan's face always reminded me, for some reason, of a smorgasbord tray.

"Did you bring your nose?" I asked, leading him over to the chemical bench.

"Yessir."

"Well"—I slid back the little panel in the neck of the retort, standing at arm's length—"stick it in there."

"Oh, but I—" He looked plaintively toward Berbelot, who smiled.

"Well . . . oh!" The "Well" was diffidence, and the "Oh" was when I grabbed him by the collar and stuck his face in the warm fumes.

Cogan went limp and stiffened so fast that he didn't move. He rose slowly, as if the power of that mighty stench was lifting him by the jawbone, turned around twice with his eyes streaming, and headed for the door. He walked lightly and slowly on the balls of his feet, with his arms bent and half raised, like a somnambulist. He walked smack into the doorpost, squeaked, said "oh . . . my . . . goodness—" faintly, and disappeared into the corridor.

"Well," said Berbelot pensively. "I really think that that stuff smells bad."

"Seems as though," I grinned. "I . . . oh, boy!" I ran to the retort and closed the slide. "Good gosh! Did we give him a concentrated shot of *that?*"

"You did."

It permeated the room, and of all malodorous effluvia, it was the most noisome. It was rotten celery, than which there is no more sickening smell in nature. It was rancid butter. It was bread-mold. It was garlic garnishing fermented Limburger. It was decay. It was things running around on six legs, mashed. It was awful.

"Berbelot," I gasped, "you don't want to kill the Breather."

"It won't kill him. He just won't like it."

"Check. *Whew!*" I mopped my face. "Now how are you going to get it up to the Ether Breather?"

"Well, we'll use the olfactometer on it," he said.

"What's that?"

"Trade gadget. I knocked it together years ago.

Without it I wouldn't have made a cent in this business." He led me over to a stand on which was an enormously complicated machine, all glittering relays and electratomic bridges. "Good heavens!" I said. "What does it do—play music?"

"Maybe you wondered why I could reel off so much about the wave theory of sensory perception," he said. "Look—see these dials? And this sensitized knob?"

"Yeah?"

"That fist size, faceted knob has each of its twelve hundred and two sides coated with a different chemical reagent, very sensitive. I drop it into a smell—"

"You *what?*"

"You heard me. An odor is an emanation of gases from the smellable specimen, constituting a loss of mass of about one fifty-billionth in a year, more or less, depending on the strength of the odor and the consistency of the emanating body. Now, I expose this knob to our Cogan-crusher"—he walked over to the retort with the knob in his hand, trailing its cable, and slid the panel back a bit—"and the gas touches every surface. Each reacts if it can. The results are collected, returned to the olfactometer, translated into a number on the big dial."

"And that is—"

"The ratio I spoke to you about. See . . . the dial reads just 786. With the frequency to abstract thought set arbitrarily, at one thousand, we have a ratio between this smell and thought."

"Take it easy, Berbelot. I'm a layman."

He smiled. "That gives us an equation to work with. 786 is to 1000 as x is to our polychrome wave."

"Isn't that a little like mixing liquor?" I said. "One set of figures is in thought vibrations, the other in radio waves."

"Ratios are like that," he reminded me. "I can have one third as many apples as you have oranges, no matter how many or how few oranges you have."

"I consider myself stood in the corner," I said. "By golly, with that gadget, no wonder your perfumes are practically a monopoly nowadays. Would it be giving away a trade secret to tell me what went into that *Doux Rêves* of yours? How on Earth did you figure out that odor? It'll make a ninety-year-old woman put on lipstick and a centenarian buy spats."

He laughed. "Sure, I'll tell you. *Doux Rêves* is 789.783 on that dial, which happens to be the smell of a rich juicy steak! But they don't associate it with steak when they buy it—at three hundred an ounce. It just smells like something desirable."

"Berbelot, you're chiseling the public."

"Mmmm-hm. That's why I pay half a billion in income tax every year. Get over on that bench."

"In front of the receiver? What are you going to do?"

"Oh, I'll have to be over here by the transmitter. I've got to adjust a carrier wave that will have the right ratio to the polychrome wave. Don't turn on the receiver yet."

I sat down. This amazing man was about to pull something unheard of. I didn't feel comfortable about it, either. How could he be so confident? He didn't know much about the Breather, any more than I did. He was acting like a man in perfect control of everything—which he was—who didn't have to worry about taking a rap for what he was about to do. Well, he built that smell, didn't he? I didn't. I could always blame him for it, even if I was the instigator. I remember wondering if I'd be able to convince the Ether Breather of that, in case the Breather got tough. Oh, well.

"O.K., Hamilton, Turn her on!"

I did so, and a few seconds later the transmitting floods clicked on. From the suspended bank of cells came a hum as soft as their soft glow. The screen flickered and cleared, and I saw myself in it, almost as if I were looking into a mirror, except that my image was not reversed. "O.K., Berbelot."

"Right. Here goes a shot of Berbelot's *Essence of Evil!*"

I heard a switch click and then the faint grate of a

rheostat. I stared at my image and my image stared back, and Berbelot came and stood where he could see me. It was only later that I remembered noticing that he was careful to stand out of range of the transmitter. The image didn't change—each tiny movement was mine, each facial twist, each—

"Look!" snapped Berbelot, and faded back to his switchboard again.

For a moment I didn't notice anything in particular, and then I saw it, too. The smallest possible twitching of the nostrils. A sudden little movement of the head. And then a just audible sniffing through the speaker. As suddenly the movement stopped.

"You got something that time, Berbelot," I yelped, "but it seems to have gone away again. The image is true."

"Splendid!" said the old man. He clicked off the transmitter and the receiving screen glowed blankly. "Now listen. I only gave it about as much as we got a few minutes ago when you left the slide open. This time I'm going to give it what you gave poor Cogan!"

"My gosh! What am I supposed to do?"

"Sit tight! If and when the Breather starts kicking, give it right back to him. Don't admit that we did it to coax him back, or, being what he ... it ... is, he'll just get coy and disappear again."

"I think you're right. Want me to get him real mad, then?"

"For a while. Then we'll sign off and go to work on him tomorrow. After a bit we'll tell him the whole story; he'll think it's funny. Having fun seems to be his reason for living—if you can call that supercosmic existence living. Then he'll be appeased. Y'know Hamilton, if we get him running errands for us he might make us a nice piece of change. We could buy up an advertising agency and have him blank out all competition with his typically wise-guy sort of interference, for instance."

"You think of everything! All right, let's go!"

The floods and cells lit up again, and in a few seconds I was staring at myself in the screen. It made me feel a little queasy. There I was looking at myself, looking at myself, looking at myself, as it were. It dizzied me.

The rheostat twirled over, and an auxiliary somewhere deep in the complicated transmitter moaned quietly. For about five minutes I strained my eyes, but not by the slightest sign did my image show that it sensed anything off-color.

"Are you sure your gadgets are working all right?" I asked Berbelot.

"Absolutely. Nothing yet? I'll be darned. Wait. A little more juice here, and I think I can build that smell up a—"

"What goes on here?" roared the speaker.

I stared. I was still seated, but my image was rising slowly. One odd thing about it—when it had been my true image, it showed me from the waist up. As it rose from the bench in the picture, it had no legs. Apparently the breather could only distort just those waves that were transmitted. A weird sight.

I'd never have known that as my face. It was twisted, and furious, and altogether unpleasant.

"Are you doing that, punk?" it asked me.

"Wh-what?"

"Don't be like that," whispered Berbelot. He was off to one side, staring entranced and exultant into the receiver. "Give'm hell, Ham!" I drew a deep breath. "Am I doing what, and who's a punk?" I asked the receiver pugnaciously.

"That stink, and you are."

"Yeah, I'm doing it, and who are you to call me one?"

"Well, cut it out, and who do I look like?"

"I wish you boys would have one conversation at a time," said Berbelot.

"None of your lip, pantywaist," I told the Breather, "or I'll come out there and plaster your shadow with substance."

"Wise guy, huh? Why, you insignificant nematode!"

"You etheric regurgitation!"

"You little quadridimensional stinkpot!"

"You faceless, formless, fightless phantasm!" I was beginning to enjoy this.

"Listen, mug, if you don't stop that business of smelling up my environment I'll strain you through a sheet of plate glass."

"Try it and I'll knock you so flat you'll call a plane a convex hemisphere."

"If you had the guts that God gave a goose, you'd come up here and fight me."

"If you weren't about as dangerous as a moth on a battle cruiser, you'd come down here and fight."

"Touché," said Berbelot.

"Oh, yeah?" said Breather.

"Yeah."

"Cliché," said Berbelot.

"I don't like your face," said the Breather.

"Take it off then."

"Not as long as I can insult you by making you look at it."

"It's more of a face to brag about than you got."

"Why, you hair-mantled, flint-hurling, aboriginal anthropophagus!"

Berbelot clicked off both transmitter and receiver. It was only then that I realized the Breather had made me see red. I was in the laboratory, on my feet, all set to take a swing at a thousand-dollar television set.

"What'd you do that for?" I snapped, turning on Berbelot.

"Easy, lad, easy!" he laughed. "The Breather's had enough, in the first place. In the second place, he was quoting Carlyle, an ancient seventeenth or eighteenth century author. You ran him plumb out of originality. You did fine!"

"Thanks," I said, wiping my fevered brow. "Think he was sore?"

"I gathered as much. We'll work on him in the morning. I'm going to leave the smell on—just a suggestion of it, so he won't forget us."

"Don't you think he'll start messing up commercial programs again?"

"No. He knows where the trouble is coming from. He's too sore just now to think of anything but that source. He might think of the commercials later on, but if there's any danger of that we'll wise him up and laugh the whole thing off."

"Darned if you don't get me into the doggonedest things," I said wonderingly.

He chuckled, and slapped me on the back. "Go on upstairs and get Cogan to feed you. I'll be along soon; I have some work to do. You're spending the night here, my boy."

I thanked him and went upstairs. I should have gone home.

I was dog tired, but before I thought of going to bed I had some figuring to do. It has been a delicious meal, though from the way Cogan acted I thought dark thoughts about arsenic in the coffee and/or a knife in the back. But the room he had shown me to was a beauty. Berbelot, as I should have expected, was as good at decorating as he was at anything else. The place was finished in chrome and gray and black, the whole thing centering around a huge mirror at one end. Building a room around a mirror is the most complimentary thing a host can do in a guest room.

It was a fascinating mirror, too. It wasn't exactly silvered—it was of a dull gray sheen, like rough-finished stainless steel. And whether it was metal or glass I couldn't tell. It gave a beautiful image—deep and true, and accentuating natural color. Probably something he "knocked together" himself.

I walked up and down absently, thinking about Berbelot and the Breather. They had a lot in common. No one could tell exactly what they were, or how great, or how powerful. Thinking about the Breather's series of cracks at me, I realized that he, or it, had spoken exactly in my idiom. Berbelot did that, too. And yet I knew that both of them could have completely swamped me with dialectical trickery.

My shadow caught my eye and I amused myself for a moment by making shadows on the wall opposite the mirror. A bird—a cat—a funny face. I'd done it ever since I was a kid and the thing fascinated me. I was pretty good at it. I wandered around the room making shadow pictures on the wall and thinking about the Breather and Berbelot, and then found myself looking into that deep mirror.

"Hi!" I said to my reflection.

It looked out at me placidly. Not a bad-looking guy, in a pair of Berbelot's cellusilk pajamas and that cocky expression. That was quite a mirror. What was it that made a guy look different? The color trick? Not entirely. Let's see. I stuck out my tongue and so did my reflection. I thumbed my nose, and turned cold inside. I knew now what it was.

The image was—not reversed.

I stood there with my right arm up, my right thumb to my nose. The reflection's right arm—the one toward my left, since it was facing me—was raised, and it thumbed its nose. I was white as a sheet.

Was I bats? Did I have a mental hangover from seeing that unreversed image in the television set downstairs?

"This is awful," I said.

It couldn't be a mirror. Not even Berbelot could build a—or was it a mirror? A—a television screen? Couldn't be—not with the depth it had. It was almost as if I were standing in front of a glass cabinet, looking at me inside. The image was three dimensional. I suddenly decided I had been thumbing my nose long enough. This must be some trick of that old devil's, I thought. No wonder he didn't have dinner with me. He was rigging up this gadget while I was eating. If it *was* a television screen—and I'd never heard of one like this—then that thing in there wasn't me—it was the Ether Breather. I listened carefully, and sure enough, heard the hum of transmitting cells. What a gag! There were cells somewhere hidden in this room sending my image away and returning it by wire! But that screen—

My reflection suddenly set its legs apart and put its hands on its hips. "What are you looking at?" it asked me.

"N-nothing," I said as sarcastically as I could while my teeth were chattering. "The Breather again, huh?"

"That's right. My, but you're ugly."

"Mind your tongue!" I said sharply. "I can switch you off, you know."

"Heh!" he jeered. "I don't have to be afraid of that any more, thanks to a trick you just showed me."

"Yeah? You can't kid me, bud. You're just some amoral cosmic ray's little accident."

"I warn you, don't get tough with me."

"I'll do what I please. You couldn't pull your finger out of a tub of lard," I euphemized.

He sighed. "O.K. You asked for it."

And then I had to live through the worst thing that any poor mortal in the history of the world ever experienced. It's one thing to have an argument with yourself in the mirror. It's something entirely different to have your reflection reach out a leg, kick down the mirror with a shattering crash, walk up to you and belt you in the mouth a couple of times before it smears you on the carpet with a terrific right hook. That's what happened to me. Just that, so help me, Hannah.

I lay there on the rug looking up at me, which had just socked I, and I said "Whooie!" and went to sleep.

I've no idea how long I lay there. When light glimmered into my jarred brain again, Berbelot was kneeling beside me chafing my wrists. The beautiful mirror—or whatever the devil it was—was in some thousand-odd pieces on the floor, and I had gone to about as many pieces psychically. I finally realized that Berbelot was saying something.

"Hamilton! What happened? What happened? Do you realize you just busted thirty thousand dollars' worth of apparatus? What's the matter with you . . . are you sick?"

I rolled over and sat up, then went hand over hand up Berbelot until I was standing beside him. My head felt like a fur-lined ball of fire and every time my heart beat it blinded me.

"What did you wreck that receiver for?" Berbelot said irascibly.

"Me wreck it? Me didn't wreck it . . . I wrecked it," I said groggily. "I was standing in front of the mirror when who should kick it down and poke me but myself"—I shook my head and let the pain of it shake my carcass—"Ow! *Whew*. I was just—"

"Stop it!" Berbelot snapped.

Almost suddenly I recovered. "Receiver . . . what do you mean receiver?"

Berbelot was hopping mad. "The new job," he shouted, pointing at the debris. "My first three-dimensional television receiver!"

"Three . . . what are you talking about, man?"

He calmed down the way he invariably did when he was asked a question about television. "It's a box of tiny projectors," he said. "They're set . . . studded . . . inside that closet affair behind the screen you just broke. The combined beams from them give a three-dimensional, or stereoscopic, effect. And now you've gone and wrecked my screen," he wailed. "Why were you ever born? Why must I suffer so because of you? Why—"

"Wait a minute, Pop—hold on there. I didn't bust your precious screen."

"You just said you did."

"Mmm-mm. So help me. It was the Breather. I had a little argument with him and he kicked down the screen and came out and beat the stern off me."

"What?" Berbelot was really shocked this time. "You're a gibbering maniac! That was your own image! You were broadcast and your image reproduced there!"

"You're a muddy-headed old stink-merchant!" I bellowed. "I suppose I kicked down your mirror, put three teeth on hinges, and then knocked myself colder'n a cake of carbonice just for a chance to lie to you!"

"This is what comes of getting an overgrown cretin

to help out in an experiment," moaned Berbelot. "Don't try my patiece any more, Hamilton!"

"*Your* patience? What the hell was that new-fangled set doing in this room anyway?"

He grinned weakly. "Oh—that. Well, I just wanted to have some fun with you. After you left I tuned in on the Breather and told him to stand by; I'd put him in touch with . . . with the guy that was smelling up his world."

"You old crumb! Fun! You wanted me to argue with that misplaced gamma-particle all night, hey? Why, I ought to . . . I think I will at that!" And I grabbed him by the neck.

"Allow *me*," said a voice behind us, and we were seized, each by a shoulder. Then our heads were cracked violently together and we found ourselves groveling at the feet of my spittin' image. Berbelot looked up at my erstwhile reflection in silent awe.

"Where were you?" I growled.

"In the corner," he said, throwing a thumb over his shoulder. "You're a pretty-looking pair, I must say."

"Berbelot," I said, "meet your Ether Breather. Now I'm going to stand on your face until you eat the shoes off my feet, because you called me a liar."

Berbelot said, "Well, I'm damned!"

The Breather remarked quietly, "You two better explain yourselves in a hysterical hurry. Otherwise I shall most certainly take you apart and put you together again, alternating the pieces."

"Oh, we were just trying to get in contact with you again."

"What for?"

"We were interested in you. We talked to you a year or so ago and then you disappeared. We wanted to talk to you again." In spite of my anger at him I found something else to admire Berbelot for. He had remembered the Breather's peculiar childishness and was using it just when somebody had to do something, quickly.

"But you told me to stop interfering!" Presto—the

creature was already plaintive, on the amicable defensive. Its mutability was amazing.

"He told you," Berbelot snorted, indicating me, where I rolled and moaned over my twice-bruised sconce. "I didn't."

"Don't you speak for each other, then? We do."

"You—singular and plural—are a homogeneous being. All humanity is not blessed with my particularly affable nature."

"Why you old narcissist!" I snorted, and lunged at him. For every inch of my lunge the Breather calmly kicked me back a foot. I did some more moaning.

"You mean you are my friend and he is not?" said the Breather, staring at me coldly as one does at a roach which is going to be stepped on if and when it moves out from the wall.

"Oh, I wouldn't go so far as to say that," said Berbelot kindly.

I had an inspiration which, for all I know, saved my life. "You said you learned from me how to come out of the television set!" I blurted.

"True. I should be grateful for that, I suppose. I shall not tear you in little pieces." He turned to Berbelot. "I heard your call, of course, but being told once was enough for me. I did not understand. When I say anything I generally mean it. Humans are not understandable, but they are very funny."

The scientist in Berbelot popped up. "What was that you said about Hamilton showing you how to come out of the set?"

"Oh, I was watching him from the screen over there. I am sorry I broke it. He was walking around the room making pictures on the walls with shadows. That's what I am doing now."

"Shadow pictures?"

"Certainly. I am a creature living in five dimensions and aware of four, just as you live in four dimensions and are aware of three. He made three-dimensional shadows that were projected on a two-dimensional surface. I am making four-dimensional pictures that are being projected in three dimensions."

Berbelot frowned. "On what surface?"

"On that of your fourth dimension, of course."

"Our fourth. Hm-m-m . . . with what light source?"

"A five-dimensional one just as your Sun, for instance, has four."

"How many dimensions are there altogether?"

"How high is up?" twinkled the Breather.

"Could I project myself into your world?"

"I don't know. Maybe . . . maybe not. Are you going to stop making that awful smell?" he said suddenly.

"Of course! We only made it to get you angry enough to come to us for a talk. We didn't mean anything by it."

"Oh!" squealed the Ether Breather delightedly. "A joke! Fun!"

"Told you he'd take it well," murmured Berbelot.

"Yeah . . . suppose he hadn't? You're a rat, Berbelot. You made darn sure that if someone had to take a rap from this aeration here, it wouldn't be you. Nice guy." There was a strained silence for a while, and then I grinned. "Aw, hell, you had it doped out, Berbelot. Shake. I'd have done the same if I had the brains."

"He isn't bad at all, is he?" asked the Breather in surprise, staring at me.

"Well, is everything all right now, Breather? Do you feel that you're welcome to come any time you wish?"

"Yes . . . yes, I think so. But I won't come this way again. I can only take form in that lovely new three-dimensional machine of yours, and I have to break a screen to get out. I am sorry. I'll talk to you any time, though. And may I do something for you sometime?"

"Why should you?" I piped up glumly.

"Oh, think of the *fun* we'll have!"

"Would you really like to do something for us?"

"Oh, yes. Please."

"Can you direct that interference of yours into any radio frequency at any time?"

"Sure."

"Now look. We are going to start a company to advertise certain products. There are other companies in the same business. Will you leave our programs strictly alone and have all the fun you want with our competitors?"

"I'd love that!"

"That will be splendid!"

"Berbelot, we're rich!"

"You're rich," he corrected gleefully, "I'm richer!"

When this was written, I had the bad habit of running out all my copy in one draft, without a carbon. As a result, there were actually a half-dozen stories which I forgot entirely. Some appeared during the war when I was out of the country and could not get copies. When I returned I spent many a narcissistic night in reading my own stuff. It was with great joy that I ran across this one; I had absolutely no recollection whatever of having written it. I wandered around for days murmuring, "Did I write BRAT? Did I really?"

Brat

"It's strictly a short-order proposition," said Michaele, tossing her searchlight hair back on her shoulders. "We've got to have a baby eight days from now or we're out a sweet pile of cash."

"We'll get one somewhere. Couldn't we adopt one or something?" I said, plucking a stalk of grass from the bank of the brook and jamming it between my front teeth.

"Takes weeks. We could kidnap one, maybe."

"They got laws. Laws are for the protection of people."

"Why does it always have to be other people?" Mike was beginning to froth up. "Shorty, get your bulk up off the ground and think of something."

"Think better this way," I said. "We could borrow one."

"Look," said Mike. "When I get my hands on a kid, that child and I have to go through a short but rigorous period of training. It's likely to be rough. If I had a baby and someone wanted to borrow it for any such purpose, I'd be damned if I'd let it go."

"Oh, you wouldn't be too tough," I said. "You've got maternal instincts and stuff."

"Shorty, you don't seem to realize that babies are very delicate creatures and require the most skilled and careful handling. I don't know *anything* about them. I am an only child, and I went right from high school into business college and from there into an office. The only experience I ever had with a baby was once when I minded one for an afternoon. It cried all the time I was there."

"Should've changed its diapers."

"I did."

"Must've stuck it with a pin then."

"I did not! You seem to know an awful lot about children," she said hotly.

"Sure I do. I was one myself once."

"Heel!" She leaped on me and rolled me into the brook. I came up spluttering and swearing. She took me by the neck, pulled me half up on the bank and began thudding my head on the soft bank.

"Let go my apple," I gasped. "This is no choking matter."

"Now will you co-operate? Shorty, quit your kidding. This is serious. Your Aunt Amanda has left us thirty grand, providing we can prove to her sister Jonquil that we are the right kind of people. 'Those who can take care of a baby can take care of money,' she used to say. We've got to be under Jonquil's eye for thirty days and take care of a baby. No nursemaids, no laundresses, no nothing."

"Let's wait till we have one of our own."

"Don't be supid! You know as well as I do that that money will set you up in a business of your own as well as paying off the mortgage on the shack. *And* decorating it. *And* getting us a new car."

"*And* a fur coat. *And* a star sapphire. Maybe I'll even get a new pair of socks."

"*Shorty!*" A full lip quivered, green eyes swam.

"Oh, darling, I didn't mean—Come here and be kissed."

She did. Then she went right on where she had left off. She's like that. She can puddle up at the drop of a cynicism, and when I apologize she sniffs once and the tears all go back into her eyes without being used. She holds them for when they'll be needed instead of wasting them. "But you know perfectly well that unless we get our hands on money—lots of it—and darn soon, we'll lose that little barn and the garage that we built just to *put* a new car in. Wouldn't that be silly?"

"No. No garage, no need for a car. Save lots of money!"

"Shorty—please."

"All right, all right. The fact that everything you say is correct doesn't help to get us a baby for thirty days. Damn money anyway! Money isn't everything!"

"Of course it isn't, darling," said Michaele sagely, "but it's what you buy everything with."

A sudden splash from the brook startled us. Mike screamed. "Shorty—grab him!"

I plunged into the water and hauled out a very tiny, very dirty—baby. It was dressed in a tattered romper, and it had an elfin face, big blue eyes and a golden topknot. It looked me over and sprayed me—*b-b-b-b-b-br-r-r*—with a combination of a mouthful of water and a Bronx cheer.

"Oh, the poor darling little angel!" said Mike. "Give him to me, Shorty! You're handling him like a bag of sugar!"

I stepped gingerly out of the brook and handed him over. Michaele cradled the filthy mite in her arms, completely oblivious to the child's effect on her white linen blouse. The same white linen blouse, I reflected bitterly, that I had been kicked out of the house for, when I pitched some cigar ashes on it. It made me feel funny, watching Mike handle that kid. I'd never pictured her that way.

The baby regarded Mike gravely as she discoursed to it about a poor drowned woofum-wuffums, and did the bad man treat it badly, then. The baby belched eloquently.

"He belches in English!" I remarked.

"Did it have the windy ripples?" cooed Mike. "Give us a kiss, honey lamb."

The baby immediately flung its little arms around her neck and planted a whopper on her mouth.

"Wow!" said Mike when she got her breath. "Shorty, could you take lessons!"

"Lessons my eye," I said jealously. "Mike, that's no baby, that's some old guy in his second childhood."

"The idea." She crooned to the baby for a moment, and then said suddenly. "Shorty—what were we talking about before heaven opened up and dropped this little bundle of—" Here the baby tried to squirm out of her arms and she paused to get a better grip.

"Bundle of what?" I asked, deadpan.

"Bundle of joy."

"Oh! Bundle of joy. What were we talking about? Ba—Hey! Babies!"

"That's right. And a will. And thirty grand."

I looked at the child with new eyes. "Who do you think belongs to the younker?"

"Someone who apparently won't miss him if we take him away for thirty days," she said. "No matter what bungling treatment I give him, it's bound to be better than what he's used to. Letting a mere baby crawl around in the woods! Why, it's awful!"

"The mere babe doesn't seem to mind" I said. "Tell you what we'll do—we'll take care of him for a few days and see if anyone claims him. We'll listen to the radio and watch the papers and the ol' grapevine. If anybody does claim him, maybe we can make a deal for a loan. At any rate we'll get to work on him right away."

At this juncture the baby eeled out of Mike's arms and took off across the grass. "Sweet Sue! Look at him go!" she said, scrambling to her feet. "Get him, Shorty!"

The infant, with twinkling heels, was crawling—running, on hands and knees—down toward the brook. I headed him off just as he reached the water, and snagged him up by the slack of his pants. As he came up off the ground he scooped up a handful of mud and pitched it into my eyes. I yelped and dropped him. When I could see a little daylight again I beheld Michaele taking a running brodie into a blackberry bush. I hurried over there, my eyelids making a nasty grating sound. Michaele was lying prone behind the baby, who was also lying prone, his little heels caught tightly in Mike's hands. He was nonchalantly picking blackberries.

Mike got to her knees and then her feet under her, and picked up the baby, who munched contentedly. "I'm disgusted with you," she said, her eyes blazing. "Flinging an innocent child around like that! Why, it's a wonder you didn't break every bone in his poor little body!"

"But I—He threw mud in my—"

"Pick on someone your size, you big bully! I never knew till now that you were a sadist with an inferiority complex."

"And I never knew till now that it's true what they say about the guy in the three-cornered pants—the king can do no wrong! What's happened to your sense of justice, woman? That little brat there—"

"Shorty! Talking that way about a poor little baby! He's beautiful! He didn't mean anything by what he did. He's too young to know any better."

In the biggest, deepest bass voice I have ever heard, the baby said, "Lady, I do know what I'm doin'. I'm old enough!"

We both sat down.

"Did you say that?" Mike wanted to know.

I shook my head dazedly.

"Coupla dopes," said the baby.

"Who—What are you?" asked Mike breathlessly.

"What do I look like?" said the baby, showing his teeth. He had very sharp, very white teeth—two on the top gum and four on the lower.

"A little bundle of—"

"Shorty!" Mike held up a slim finger.

"Never mind him," growled the child. "I know lots of four-letter words. Go ahead, bud."

"You go ahead. What are you—a midget?"

I no sooner got the second syllable of that word out when the baby scuttled over to me and rocked my head back with a surprising right to the jaw. "That's the last time I'm going to be called that by anybody!" He roared deafeningly. "No! I'm not a . . . a . . . what you said. I'm a pro tem changeling, and that's all."

"What on earth is that?" asked Mike.

"Just what I said!" snapped the baby, "a pro tem changeling. When people treat their babies too well—or not well enough—I show up in their bassinets and give their folks what for. Only I'm always the spitting image of their kid. When they wise up in the treatment, they get their kids back—not before."

"Who pulls the switch? I mean, who do you work for?"

The baby pointed to the grass at our feet. I had to look twice before I realized what he was pointing at. The blades were dark and glossy and luxuriant in a perfect ring about four feet in diameter.

Michaele gasped and put her knuckles to her lips. "The Little People!" she breathed.

I was going to say, "Don't be silly, Mike!" but her taut face and the baby's bland, nodding head stopped me.

"Will you work for us?" she asked breathlessly. "We need a baby for thirty days to meet the conditions of a will."

"I heard you talking about it," said the baby. "No."

"No?"

"No."

A pause. "Look, kid," I said, "what do you like? Money? Food? Candy? Circuses?"

"I like steaks," said the child gruffly. "Rare, fresh, thick. Onions. Cooked so pink they say, 'Moo!' when you bite 'em. Why?"

"Good," I said. "If you work for us, you'll get all the steaks you can eat."

"No."

"What would you want to work for us?"

"Nothin'. I don't wanna work for you."

"What are we going to do?" I whispered to Mike. "This would be perfect!"

"Leave it to me. Look—baby—what's your name, anyway?"

"Percival. But don't call me Percival! Butch."

"Well, look, Butch; we're in an awful jam. If we don't get hold of a sockful of money darn soon, we'll lose that pretty little house over there."

"What's the matter with *him*? Can't he keep up the payments? What is he—a bum?"

"Hey, you—"

"Shut up, Shorty. He's just beginning, Butch. He's a graduate caterer. But he has to get a place of his own before he can make any real money."

"What happens if you lose th' house?"

"A furnished room. The two of us."

"What's the matter with that?"

I tensed. This was a question I had asked her myself.

"Not for me. I just couldn't live that way." Mike would wheedle, but she wouldn't lie.

Butch furrowed his nonexistent eyebrows. "Couldn't? Y' know, I like that. High standards." His voice deepened; the question lashed her. "Would you live with him in a furnished room if there were no other way?"

"Well, of course."

"I'll help you," said Butch instantly.

"Why?" I asked. "What do you expect to get out of it?"

"Nothing—some fun, maybe. I'll help you because you need help. That's the only reason I ever do anything for anybody. That's the only thing you should have told me in the first place—that you were in a jam. You and your bribes!" he snapped at me, and turned to Mike. "I ain't gonna like that guy," he said.

I said, "I already don't like you."

As we started back to the house, Butch said, "But I'm gonna get my steaks?"

Aunt Jonquil's house stood alone in a large lot with its skirts drawn primly up and an admonishing expression on its face. It looked as if it had squeezed its way between two other houses to hide itself, and some scoundrel had taken the other houses away.

And Aunt Jonquil, like her house, was five times as high as she was wide, extremely practical, unbeautifully ornate, and stood alone. She regarded marriage as an unfortunate necessity. She herself never married because an unkind nature had ruled that she must marry a man, and she thought that men were uncouth. She disapproved of smoking, drinking, swearing, gambling, and loud laughter. Smiles she enjoyed only if she could fully understand what was being smiled at; she mistrusted innuendo. A polite laugh was a thing she permitted herself perhaps twice a week, providing it was atoned for by ten minutes of frozen-face gravity. Added to which, she was a fine person. Swell.

On the way to the city, I sat through this unnerving conversation.

Butch said, "Fathead! Drive more carefully!"

"He's doing all right," said Mike. "Really. It surprises me. He's usually an Indian." She was looking very lovely in a pea-green linen jacket and a very simple white skirt and a buff straw hat that looked like a halo.

Butch was wearing a lace-edged bonnet and an evil gleam in his eye to offset the angelic combination of a pale-blue sweater with white rabbits applied on the sides, and fuzzy Angora booties on which he had insisted because I was wearing a navy-blue and he knew it would come off all over me. He was, I think, a little uncomfortable due to my rather unskilled handling of his diapering. And the reason for my doing that job was to cause us more trouble than a little bit. Butch's ideas of privacy and the proprieties were advanced. He would no more think of letting Mike bathe or change him than I would think of letting Garbo change me. Thinking about this, I said:

"Butch, that prudishness of yours is going to be tough to keep up at Aunt Jonquil's."

"You'll keep it up, son." said the infant, "or I'll quit working. I ain't going to have no women messin' around me that way. What d'ye think I am—an exhibitionist?"

"I think you're a liar," I said. "And I'll tell you why. You said you made a life's work of substituting for children. How could you with ideas like that? Who you trying to horse up?"

"Oh," said Butch, "that. Well, I might's well confess to you that I ain't done that kind of work in years. I got sick of it. I was gettin' along in life and ... well, you can imagine. Well, about thutty years ago I was out of a job an' the woman was changing my drawers when a half-dozen babes arrived from her sewin' circle. She left off workin' right where she was and sang out for them all to come in and see how pretty I looked the way I was. I jumped out o' th' bassinet, grabbed a diaper off th' bed an' held it in front of me while I called the whole bunch of 'em what they were and told them to get out of there. I got fired for it. I thought they'd put me to work hauntin' houses or cleanin' dishes for sick people or somethin', but no—they cracked down on me. Told me I'd have to stay this way until I was repentant."

"Are you?" giggled Mike.

Butch snorted. "Not so you'd notice it," he growled. "Repentant because I believe in common decency? Heh?"

We waited a long time after we rang the bell before Jonquil opened the door. That was to give her time to peep out at us from the tumorous bay window and compose her features to meet the niece by marriage her unfastidious nephew had acquired.

"Jonquil!" I said heartily, dashing forward and delivering the required peck on her cheek. Jonquil expected her relatives to use her leathery cheek precisely as she herself used a napkin. Pat. Dry surface on dry surface. Moisture is vulgar.

"And this is Michaele," I said, stepping aside.

Mike said, "How do you do?" demurely, and smiled.

Aunt Jonquil stepped back a pace and held her head as if she were sighting at Mike through her nostrils. "Oh, yes," she said without moving her lips. The smile disappeared from Mike's face and came back with an effort of will that hurt. "Come in," said Jonquil at last, and with some reluctance.

We trailed through a foyer and entered the parlor. It wasn't a living room, it was an honest-to-goodness front parlor with antimacassars and sea shells. The tone of the room was sepia—light from the background of the heavily flowered wallpaper, dark for the furniture. The chairs and a hard-looking divan were covered with a material that looked as if it had been bleeding badly some months ago. When Butch's eye caught the glassed-in monstrosity of hay and dead flowers over the mantelpiece, he retched audibly.

"What a lovely place you have here," said Mike.

"Glad you like it," acknowledged Jonquil woodenly. "Let's have a look at the child." She walked over and peered at Butch. He scowled at her. "Good heavens!" she said.

"Isn't he lovely?" said Mike.

"Of course," said Jonquil without enthusiasm, and added, after searching her store of ready-made expressions, "the little wudgums!" She kitchy-cooed his chin with her sharp forefinger. He immediately began to wail, with the hoarse, high-pitched howl of a genuine baby.

"The poor darling's tired after his trip," said Mike.

Jonquil, frightened by Butch's vocal explosion, took the hint and led the way upstairs.

"Is the whole damn house like this?" whispered Butch hoarsely.

"No. I don't know. Shut up," said Mike. My sharp-eared aunt swiveled on the steps. "And go to sleepy-bye," she crooned aloud. She bent her head over his and hissed, "And keep on crying, you little wretch!"

Butch snorted and then complied.

We walked into a bedroom, austerely furnished, the kind of room they used in the last century for sleeping purposes only, and therefore designed so that it was quite unattractive to anyone with anything but sleep on his mind. It was all gray and white; the only spot of color in the room was the bedstead, which was a highly polished pipe organ. Mike laid the baby down on the bed and stripped off his booties, his shirt and his sweater. Butch put his fist in his mouth and waited tensely.

"Oh—I almost forgot. I have the very same bassinet you used, up in the attic," said Jonquil. "I should have had it ready. Your telegram was rather abrupt, Horace. You should have let me know sooner that you'd come today." She angled out of the room.

"Horace! I'll be—Is your name Horace?" asked Butch in delight.

"Yes," I said gruffly. "But it's Shorty to you, see, little man?"

"And I was worried about you callin' me Percival!"

I helped set up the bassinet and we tucked Butch in for his nap. I managed to be fooling around with his bedclothes when Mike bent over dutifully to give him a kiss. I grabbed Butch's chin and held it down so the kiss landed on his forehead. He was mightily wroth, and bit my finger till it bled. I stuck it in my pocket and told him, "I'll see you later, bummy-wummy!" He made a noise, and Jonquil fled, blushing.

We convened in the kitchen, which was far and away the pleasantest room in the house. "Where on earth did you get that child?" Jonquil asked, peering into a nice-smelling saucepan on the old-fashioned range.

"Neighbor's child," I said. "They were very poor and were glad to have him off their hands for a few weeks."

"He's a foundling," Mike ingeniously supplemented. "Left on their doorstep. He's never been adopted or anything."

"What's his name?"

"We call him Butch."

"How completely vulgar!" said Jonquil. "I will have no child named Butch in my house. We shall have to give him something more refined."

I had a brain wave. "How about Percival?" I said.

"Percival. Percy," murmered Jonquil, testing it out. "That is much better. That will do. I knew somebody called Percival once."

"Oh—you better not call him Percival," said Mike, giving me her no-good-can-come-of-this look.

"Why not?" I said blandly. "Lovely name."

"Yeah," said Mike. "Lovely."

"What time does Percival get his dinner?" asked Jonquil.

"Six o'clock."

"Good," said Jonquil. "I'll feed him!"

"Oh no, Aunt J—I mean, Miss Timmins. That's our job."

I think Jonquil actually smiled. "I think I'd like to do it," she said. "You're not making an inescapable duty out of this, are you?"

"I don't know what you mean," said Mike, a little coldly. "We *like* that child."

Jonquil peered intently at her. "I believe you do," she said in a surprised tone, and started out of the room. At the door she called back, "You needn't call me Miss Timmins," and she was gone.

"Well!" said Mike.

"Looks like you won the war, babe."

"Only the first battle, honey, and don't think I don't

know it. What a peculiar old duck she is!" She busied herself at the stove, warming up some strained carrots she had taken out of a jar, sterilizing a bottle and filling it with pineapple juice. We had read a lot of baby manuals in the last few days!

Suddenly, "Where's your aunt?" Mike asked.

"I dunno. I guess she's—Good grief!"

There was a dry-boned shriek from upstairs and then the sound of hard heels pounding along the upper hallway toward the front stairs. We went up the back stairs two at a time, and saw the flash of Jonquil's dimity skirts as she disappeared downstairs. We slung into the bedroom. Butch was lying in his bassinet doubled up in some kind of spasm.

"Now what?" I groaned.

"He's choking," said Mike. "What are we going to do, Shorty?"

I didn't know. Mike ran and turned him over. His face was all twisted up and he was pouring sweat and gasping. "Butch! Butch—What's the matter?"

And just then he got his wind back. *"Ho ho ho!"* he roared in his bullfrog voice, and lost it again.

"He's laughing!" Mike whispered.

"That's the funniest way I ever saw anyone commit sideways," I said glumly. I reached out and smacked him across the puss. "Butch! Snap out of it!"

"Ooh!" said Butch. "You lousy heel. I'll get you for that."

"Sorry, Butch. But I thought you were strangling."

"Guess I was at that," he said, and started to laugh again. "Shorty, I couldn't help it. See, that ol' vinegar visage come in here and started staring at me. I stared right back. She bends over the bassinet. I grin. She grins. I open my mouth. She opens her mouth. I reach in and pull out her bridgework and pitch it out the windy. Her face sags down in the middle like a city street in Scranton. She does the steam-siren act and hauls out o' here. But Shorty—Mike"—and he went off into another helpless spasm—"you shoulda seen her *face!*"

We all subsided when Jonquil came in again. "Just tending to my petunias," she said primly. "Why—you have dinner on the table. Thank you, child."

"Round two," I said noncommittally.

Around two in the morning I was awakened by a soft thudding in the hallway. I came up on one elbow. Mike was fast asleep. But the bassinet was empty. I breathed an oath and tiptoed out into the hall. Halfway down was Butch, crawling rapidly. In two strides I had him by the scruff of the neck.

"Awk!"

"Shut up! Where do you think you're going?"

He thumbed at a door down the hall.

"No, Butch. Get on back to bed. You can't go there."

He looked at me pleadingly. "I can't? Not for *nothin'?*"

"Not for nothin'."

"Aw—Shorty. Gimme a break."

"Break my eyebrow. You belong in that bassinet."

"Just this once, huh, Shorty?"

I looked worriedly at Jonquil's bedroom door. "All right, dammit. But make it snappy."

Butch went on strike the third day. He didn't like those strained vegetables and soups to begin with, and then one morning he heard the butcher boy downstairs, singing out, "Here's yer steaks, Miss Timmins!" That was enough for little Percival.

"There's got to be a new deal around here, chum," he said the next time he got me in the room alone. "I'm gettin' robbed."

"Robbed? Who's taking what?"

"Youse. You promise me steaks, right? Listen, Shorty, I'm through with that pap you been feedin' me. I'm starvin' to death on it."

"What would you suggest?" I asked calmly. "Shall I have one done to your taste and delivered to your room, sir?"

"You know what, Shorty? You're kiddin'." He jabbed a tiny forefinger into the front of my shirt for emphasis. "You're kiddin', but I ain't. An' what you just said is a pretty good idea. I want a steak once a day—here in this room. I mean it, son."

I opened my mouth to argue and then looked deep into those baby eyes. I saw an age-old stubbornness, an insurmountable firmness of character there. I shrugged and went out.

In the kitchen I found Mike and Jonquil deeply engaged in some apparently engrossing conversation about rayon taffeta. I broke it up by saying, "I just had an idea. Tonight I'm going to eat my supper upstairs with Bu ... Percival. I want you to get to know each other better, and I would commune with another male for a spell. I'm outnumbered down here."

Jonquil actually did smile this time. Smiles seemed to be coming to her a little more easily these days. "I think that's a lovely idea," she said. "We're having steak tonight, Horace. How do you like yours?"

"Broiled," said Mike, "and well d—"

"Rare!" I said, sending a glance at Mike. She shut up, wonderingly.

And that night I sat up in the bedroom, watching that miserable infant eat my dinner. He did it with gusto, with much smacking of the lips and grunting in ecstasy.

"What do you expect me to do with this?" I asked, holding up a cupful of lukewarm and sticky strained peas.

"I don't know," said Butch with his mouth full. "That's your problem."

I went to the window and looked out. Directly below was a spotless concrete walk which would certainly get spattered if I pitched the unappetizing stuff out there. "Butch—won't you get rid of the stuff for me?"

He sighed, his chin all greasy from my steak. "Thanks, no," he said luxuriously. "Couldn't eat another bite."

I tasted the peas tentatively, held my nose and

gulped them down. As I swallowed the last of them I found time to direct a great many highly unpleasant thoughts at Butch. "No remarks, *Percy*," I growled.

He just grinned. I picked up his plates and the cup and started out. "Haven't you forgotten something?" he asked sleepily.

"What?" He nodded toward the dresser and the bottle which stood on it. Boiled milk with water and corn syrup added. "Damned if I will!" I snapped.

He grinned, opened his mouth and started to wail.

"Shut up!" I hissed. "You'll have them women up here claiming I'm twisting your tail or something."

"That's the idea," said Butch. "Now drink your milk like a good little boy and you can go out and play."

I muttered something impotently, ripped the nipple off the bottle and gulped the contents.

"That's for telling the old lady to call me Percy," said Butch. "I want another steak tomorrow. 'Bye now."

And that's how it came about that I, a full-grown man in good health, lived for close to two weeks on baby food. I think that the deep respect I have for babies dates from this time, and is founded on my realization of how good-natured they are on the diet they get. It sure didn't work that way with me. What really griped me was having to watch him eat my meals. Brother, I was earning that thirty grand the hard way.

About the beginning of the third week Butch's voice began to change. Mike noticed it first and came and told me.

"I think something's the matter with him," she said. "He doesn't seem as strong as he was, and his voice is getting high-pitched."

"Don't borrow trouble, beautiful," I said, putting my arm around her. "Lord knows he isn't losing any weight on the diet he's getting. And he has plenty of lung power."

"That's another thing," she said in a puzzled tone. "This morning he was crying and I went in to see what he wanted. I spoke to him and shook him but he went on crying for almost five minutes before he suddenly sat up and said 'What? What? Eh—it's you, Mike.' I asked him what he wanted; he said nothing and told me to scram."

"He was kidding you."

She twisted out of my arms and looked up at me, her golden brows just touching over the snowy crevasse of her frown. "Shorty—he was crying—*real tears.*"

That was the same day that Jonquil went in to town and bought herself a half dozen bright dresses. And I strongly suspect she had something done to her hair. She looked fifteen years younger when she came in and said, "Horace—it seems to me you used to smoke."

"Well . . . yes—"

"Silly boy! You've stopped smoking just because you think I wouldn't approve! I like to have a man smoking around the house. Makes it more homey. Here."

She pressed something into my hand and fled, red-faced and bright-eyed. I looked at what she had given me. Two packs of cigarettes. They weren't my brand, but I don't think I have ever been so deeply touched.

I went and had a talk with Butch. He was sleeping lightly when I entered the room. I stood there looking down at him. He was awful tiny, I thought. I wonder what it is these women gush so much about.

Butch's eyes were so big under his lids that they seemed as if they just couldn't stay closed. The lashes lay on his cheek with the most gentle of delicate touches. He breathed evenly, with occasionally a tiny catch. It made nice listening, somehow. I caught a movement out of the corner of my eye—his hand, clenching and unclenching. It was very rosy, and far too small to be so perfect. I looked at my own hand and at his, and I just couldn't believe it . . .

He woke suddenly, opening his eyes and kicking. He looked first at the window, and then at the wall oppo-site. He whimpered, swallowed, gave a little cry. Then he turned his head and saw me. For a long moment he watched me, his deep eyes absolutely unclouded; suddenly he sat up and shook his head. "Hello," he said sleepily.

I had the strange sensation of watching a person wake up twice. I said, "Mike's worried about you," I told him why.

"Really?" he said. "I—don't feel much different. Heh! Imagine this happening to me!"

"Imagine what happening?"

"I've heard of it before, but I never . . . Shorty, you won't laugh at me, will you?"

I thought of all that baby food, and all those steaks. "Don't worry. You ain't funny."

"Well, you know what I told you about me being a changeling. Changelings is funny animals. Nobody likes 'em. They raise all kinds of hell. Fathers resent 'em because they cry all night. Mothers get panicky if they don't know it's a changeling, and downright resentful if they do. A changeling has a lot of fun bein' a brat, but he don't get much emotional sugar, if you know what I mean. Well, in my case . . . dammit, I can't get used to it! Me, of all people . . . well, someone around here . . . uh . . . loves me."

"Not me," I said quickly, backing away.

"I know, not you." He gave me a sudden, birdlike glance and said softly, "You're a pretty good egg, Shorty."

"Huh? Aw—"

"Anway, they say that if any woman loves a changeling, he loses his years and his memories, and turns into a real human kid. But he's got to be loved for himself, not for some kid he replaces." He shifted uneasily. "I don't . . . I can't get used to it happening to me, but . . . oh oh!" A pained expression came across his face and he looked at me helplessly. I took in the situation at a glance.

A few minutes later I corralled Mike. "Got something for you," I said, and handed her something made of layette cloth.

"What's . . . Shorty! Not—"

I nodded. "Butch's getting infantile," I said.

While she was doing the laundry a while later I told her what Butch had said. She was very quiet while I told her, and afterward.

"Mike—if there is anything in all this fantastic business, it wouldn't be you, would it, that's making this change in him?"

She thought it over for a long time and then said, "I think he's terribly cute, Shorty."

I swung her around. She had soapsuds on her temple, where her fingers had trailed when she tossed her bright hair back with her wrist.

"Who's the number one man around here?" I whispered. She laughed and said I was silly and stood on tiptoe to kiss me. She's a little bit of a thing.

The whole thing left me feeling awful funny.

Our thirty days were up, and we packed. Jonquil helped us, and I've never seen her so full of life. Half the time she laughed, and once in a while she actually broke down and giggled. And at lunch she said to us, "Horace—I'm afraid to let you take little Percy back with you. You said that those people who had him were sort of ne'er-do-wells, and they wouldn't miss him much. I wish you'd leave him with me for a week or so while you find out just what their home life is like, and whether they really want him back. If not, I . . . well, I'll see that he gets a good place to live in."

Mike and I looked at each other, and then Mike looked up at the ceiling, toward the bedroom. I got up suddenly. "I'll ask him," I said, and walked upstairs.

Butch was sitting up in the bassinet trying to catch a sunbeam. "Hey!" I said. "Jonquil wants you to stick around. What do you say?"

He looked at me, and his eyes were all baby, nothing else.

"Well?"

He made some tremendous mental effort, pursed his lips, took a deep breath, held it for an unconscionable time, and then one word burst out. "Percy!"

"I get it," I said. "So long, fella."

He didn't say anything; just went back to his sunbeam.

"It's O.K. with him," I said when I got back to the table.

"You never struck me as the kind of man who would play games with children," laughed Jonquil. "You'll do . . . you'll do. Michaele, dear—I want you to write to me. I'm so glad you came."

So we got our thirty grand. We wrote as soon as we reached the shack—*our* shack, now—that no, the people wouldn't want Percy back, and that his last name was—Fay. We got a telegram in return thanking us and telling us that Jonquil was adopting the baby.

"You goin' to miss ol' Butch?" I asked Mike.

"No," she said. "Not too much. I'm sort of saving up."

"Oh," I said.

The title, of course, is from the old saw about genius— "ninety-eight percent perspiration." I have since revised my conception of genius and now define it as an infinite capacity for taking beer. This story is the only one I ever wrote which has three (count 'em) plot twists at the end. I am proud of one thing in it: Satan Strong, Scourge of the Spaceways, Supporter of the Serialized Short Story, and Specialist in Science on the Spot.

Two Percent Inspiration

Dr. Bjornsen was a thorough man. He thought that way and acted that way and expected others to exceed him in thoroughness. Since this was an impossibility, he expressed an almost vicious disappointment in incompetents, and took delight in pointing out the erring one's shortcomings. He was in an ideal position for this sort of thing, being principal of the Nudnick Institute.

Endowed by Professor Thaddeus MacIlhainy Nudnick, the institute was conducted for the purpose of supplying brilliant young assistants to Professor Nudnick. It enrolled two thousand students every year, and the top three of the graduating class were given subsistence and a considerable salary for the privilege of entering Nudnick's eight-year secondary course, where they underwent some real study before they began as assistants in the Nudnick laboratories.

Bjornsen never congratulated an honor student, for they had behaved as expected. He found many an opportunity of delivering a kick or two in the slats of those who had fallen by the wayside; and of these opportunities, the ones that pleased him the most were the ones involving expulsion. He considered himself an expert disciplinarian, and he was more than proud of his forte for invective.

It was with pleasurable anticipation that he summoned one Hughie McCauley to his office one afternoon. Hughie was a second-year student, and made ideal bait for Bjornsen's particular line of attack. The kid was intelligent to a degree, and fairly well read, so that he could understand Bjornsen's more subtle insults. He was highly sensitive, so that he could be hurt by what Bjornsen said, and he showed it. He lacked sense, so that he continually retorted to Bjornsen's comments, giving the principal blurted statements to pick meticulously apart while the victim writhed. Hughie was such perfect material for persecution that Bjornsen rather hated to expel him; but he comforted himself by recalling the fact that there were hundreds of others who could be made to squirm. He'd take his time with Hughie, however; stretch it out, savor the boy's suffering before he kicked him out of the school.

"Send him in," Bjornsen told the built-in communicator on his luxurious desk. He leaned back in his chair, put the tips of his fingers together, lowered his head so that only the whites of his eyes were visible as he stared through his shaggy brows at the door, and waited.

Hughie came in, his hair plastered unwillingly down, his fear and resentment sticking out all over him. The kid's knees knocked together so that he stumbled against the doorpost. There was a gloss of cold sweat on his forehead. From previous experience, he had no difficulty in taking up the front-and-center position before the principal's desk.

"Y-yes sir!"

Bjornsen made a kissing noise with his wrinkled lips before he spoke, threw back his head and glared. "You might," he said quietly, "have washed your ears before you came in here." He knew that there is no more painfully undignified attack for an adolescent, particularly if it is not true. Hughie flushed and stuck out his lower lip.

Bjornsen said, "You are an insult to this institution. You were in a position, certainly, to know yourself before you applied for admission; therefore, the very act of applying was dishonest and insincere. You must have known that you were unfit even to enter these buildings, to say nothing of daring to perpetuate the mistake of the board of examiners in staying here. I am thoroughly disgusted with you." Bjornsen smiled his disgust, and it was a smile that perfectly matched his words. He bent to flip the switch on the communicator, cutting off its mellow buzz. "Yes?"

"Dr. Bjornsen! Professor Nudnick is—"

The annunciator's hollow voice was drowned out in the crashing of a hard, old foot against the door. Nudnick kicked it open because he knew it could not be slammed, and he liked startling Bjornsen. "What sort of nonsense is this?" he demanded, in a voice that sounded like flatulence through ten feet of lead pipe. "Since when has that vinegar-visaged female out there been instructed to announce me? Damn it, you'll see me whether you're busy or not!"

Bjornsen had bounced out of his chair to indulge in every sort of sycophantism short of curtsying. "Professor Nudick! I am delighted to see you!" This was perfect. The only thing that could possibly increase Hughie McCauley's agony was to have an audience to his dismissal; and what better audience could he have than the great endower of the school himself? Bjornsen rubbed his hands, which yielded an unpleasant dry sound, and began.

"Professor Nudick," he said, catching Hughie's trembling shoulder and using it to thrust the attached boy between him and Nudnick, "you could not have picked a better time to arrive. This shivering example of negation is typical of the trash that has been getting by the examiners recently. Now I may prove to you that my recent letter on the subject was justified.

Nudnick looked calmly at Hughie. "I don't read your letters," he said. "They bore me. What's he done?"

Bjornsen, a little taken aback, put this new resentment into his words. "Done? What he hasn't done is more important. He has neglected to tidy up his thinking habits. He indulges in reading imaginative fiction during his hours of relaxation instead of reading books pertaining in some way to his studies. He whistles in corridors. He asks impertinent questions of his instructors. He was actually discovered writing a letter to a . . . a *girl!*"

"*Tsk, tsk,*" chuckled the professor. "This during classes?"

"Certainly not! Even he would not go that far, though I expect it hourly."

"Hm-m-m. Is he intelligent?"

"Not very."

"What kind of questions does he ask?"

"Oh—stupid ones. About the nature of a spacewarp, whatever that may be, and about whether or not time travel is possible. A dreamer—that's what he is, and a scientific institution is no place for dreamers."

"What are you going to do with him?"

"Expel him, of course."

Nudnick reached over and pulled the boy out of Bjornsen's claw. "Then why not post him as expelled and spare him this agony? It so happens, Bjornsen, that this is just the kind of boy I came here to get. I'm going to take him with me on a trip to the Asteroid Belt. Salary at two thousand a month, if he's willing. Are you, what's-your-name?"

Hughie nodded swimmingly.

"Eh." Beckoning the boy, Nudnick started for the door. "My advice to you, Bjornsen," grated the scientist, "is as follows. Keep your nose out of the students' lives on their off hours. If you must continue in these little habits of yours, take it out in pulling the wings off flies. And get married. Take this advice or hand in your resignation effective this date next month."

Hughie paused at the door, looking back. Nudnick gave him a quick look, shoved him toward Bjornsen. "Go ahead, kid. I'd like it, too."

Hughie grinned, walked up to Bjornsen, and with a quick one-two knocked the principal colder than a cake of ice.

They were eight days out now, and these were the eight:

The day when the unpredictable Professor Nudnick had whisked Hughie up to his mountain laboratory, and had put him to work loading the last of an astonishingly inclusive list of stores into the good ship *Stoutfella*. Hughie began to regard the professor as a little less than the god he had imagined, and a little more as a human being. The old man was perpetually cheerful, pointing out Hughie's stupidities and his little triumphs without differentiating between them. He treated Hughie with a happy tolerance, and seemed to be more delighted with the lad's ignorance than by his comparatively meager knowledge. When Hughie had haltingly asked if he might take a suitcase full of fiction with him, Nudnick had chuckled dryly and sent him off to the nearest town with a pocketful of money. Hughie arrived back at the laboratory laden and blissful. They took off.

And the day when they heard the last broadcast news report before they whisked through the Heaviside layer, among other items was one to the effect that Dr. Emil Bjornsen, principal of the Nudnick Institute, had resigned to accept a government job. Hughie had laughed gleefully at this, but Nudnick shook his shaggy old head. "Not funny, Hughie," he said. "Bjornsen's a shrewd man. I've an idea why he did that, and it has nothing to do with my . . . our . . . ultimatum."

Struck by the scientist's sober tone, Hughie calmed down to ask, "What did he do it for?"

Nudnick clapped a perforated course card into the automatic pilot, reeled its lower edge into the integrator, and checked his controls before switching them over to the "Iron Mike."

"It has to do with this trip," he said, waving the kid into the opposite seat, "and it's about time you knew what this is all about. What we're after is a mineral deposit of incalculable value. How it is, I don't know, but somewhere in that mess of nonsense out there"—he indicated the Asteroid Belt—"is a freak. It's a lump like the rest of the asteroids, but it differs from the rest of them. It must've been a wanderer, drifting heaven alone knows how far in space until it got caught in the Belt. It's almost pure, through and through—an oxide of prosydium. That mean anything to you?"

Hughie pushed a couple of freckles together over his nose. "Yeah. Rare Earth element. Used for . . . lessee . . . something to do with Nudnick Metal, isn't it?"

"That's right: Do you know what Nudnick Metal is?"

"No. Far as I know it's a trade secret, known only to the workers in the Isopolis Laboratories." The Isopolis Laboratories were half heaven and half prison. By government grant, the great Nudnick plant there turned out the expensive metal. It was manned by workers who would never again set foot outside the walls—men who did not have to, for everything they could possibly want was supplied them. There was no secret about the way they lived, nor about anything in the fifty-square-mile enclosure except the process itself. "Nudnick's Metal is a synthetic element, thousands of times denser than anything else known. That's about all I remember," Hughie finished lamely.

Nudnick chuckled. "I'll let you in on it. The metal is the ideal substance for coating spaceships, because it's as near being impenetrable as anything in the Universe. This ship, for instance, is coated with a layer of the stuff less than one one-hundred-fifty-thousandths of an inch thick, and yet is protected against practically anything. We could run full tilt into an object the size of Earth, and though the impact would drill a molten hole thirty miles deep and most likely kill us a little bit, the hull wouldn't even be scratched. Heh. Want to know what Nudnick Metal is? I'll tell you. Copper. Just plain, ordinary, everyday Cu!"

Hughie said, "Copper? But what makes it—How is it—"

"Easy enough. You know, Hughie, it's the simple things that are really effective. Try to remember that. Nudnick Metal is *collapsed* copper; collapsed in the way that the elements of the companions of Sirius and Procyon are collapsed. You know the analogy—pile wine-glasses into a barrel, and there'll be a definite, small number of glasses that can be packed in. But crush them to fine powder, and then start packing. The barrel will hold thousands upon thousands more. The molecules of Nudnick Metal are crushed that way. You could build four hundred ships this size, from stem to stern of solid copper, and you'd use less copper than that which was used to coat this hull.

"The process is only guessed at because copper is synthesized from the uranium we ship into Isopolis ostensibly for power. As you just said, it is known that we import prosydium. That's the only clue anyone but I and the Isopolites have as to the nature of the process. But prosydium isn't an ingredient. It's more like a catalyst. Of all the elements, only prosydium can, by its atomic disintegration, absorb the unbelievable heat liberated by the collapse of the copper molecules. I won't go into the details of it, but the energy thus absorbed and transmuted can be turned back to hasten the collapsing process. The tough thing about prosydium is that it's as rare as a hairy egg, and so far no one's been able to synthesize it in usable quantities. All of which makes Nudnick Metal a trifle on the expensive side. This lump of prosydium in the Belt will cut the manufacturing cost way down, and the man or concern or planet that gets hold of it can write his—its—own ticket. See?"

"I will," said Hughie slowly, "if you'll say all that over again a few thousand times a day for the next couple of years." The boy was enormously flattered by the scientist's confiding in him. Though he himself was not qualified to use it, he knew that the information he had just received was worth countless millions in the right quarters. It frightened him a little. He wanted to keep the old man talking, and so reached for a question. "Why do we have to sneak out in a little ship like this? Why not take a flotilla of destroyers from Earth and take possession?"

"Can't do things that way, son. The Joint Patrol puts the kibosh on that. You can blame the jolly old idealism of the Interplanetary Peace Congress for that, and the Equal Armament Amendment. You see, Mars and Earth are forced by mutual agreement to maintain absolutely equal armament, to share all new developments and to police space with a Joint Patrol. A flotilla of Earth ships taking off without the knowledge or consent of the Patrol constitutes an act of war. War is a nasty business for a lot of people who weren't in on starting it. We can't do it that way. But if I turn over the location of my find to the Patrol, it becomes the property of the Joint Patrol, neatly tied up in red tape, and it doesn't do anybody any good—particularly the Nudnick Laboratories. However—here's where we come in.

"If an independent expedition lands on, or takes in tow, any body in space that is not the satellite of a planet, said body becomes the sole property of that expedition. Therefore, I've got to keep this expedition as secret from Earth as from Mars, so that Earth—and Nudnick—can get the ultimate benefit. In two months my little treasure will be in opposition with Earth. If I have taken it in tow by then, I can announce my discovery by ultraradio. The signal reaches Earth before it reaches Mars; by the time the little red men can send out a pirate to erase me, I am surrounded by a Patrol Fleet, and quite safe. But if Mars gets wind of what I am up to, son, we are going to be intercepted, followed, and rubbed out for the glory and profit of the red planet. Get it?"

"I get it. But what's all this got to do with Bjornsen?"

The old scientist scratched his nose. "I don't know. Bjornsen's a most peculiar egg, Hughie. He worked most of his life to get to be principal of the institute, and it seems to me he didn't do it just for the salary and prestige attached. More than once that egocentric martinet tried to pump me for information about what I was doing, about the Nudnick Metal process, about a hundred things of the sort. I'm sure he hasn't got any real information, but he might possibly have a hunch. A good hunch is plenty to put a Martian ship on our tail and a lot of money in Bjornsen's pocket. We'll see."

And then there was the day when Hughie had made bold enough to ask Nudnick why he had picked him for the trip, when he had his choice of thousands upon thousands of other assistants. Nudnick unwrapped his white teeth in one of his indescribable grins.

"Lots of reasons, son, among which are the fact that I delight in displeasing the contents of Bjornsen's stuffed shirt, and the fact that I dislike being bored, and since I must needs make this trip myself, I might as well be amused while I am cooped up. Also, I have found that baby geniuses are inclined to be a little cocky about what they know, and the fact that they knew it at such a tender age. A trained assistant, on the other hand, is almost certain to be a specialist of sorts, and specialists have inflexible and dogmatic minds. Bjornsen said that one of your cardinal crimes was that you relaxed in fantasy. I, with all of my scientific savvy, can find it in me to admire a mind which can conceive of the possibility of a space-warp, or time-travel. Don't look at me that way—I'm not kidding you. I can't possibly imagine such a thing—my mind is far too cluttered up with facts. I don't know whether or not a Martian ship will pick up our trail on this trip. If one does, it will take fantastic thinking to duck him. I'm incapable of thinking that way, so it's up to you."

Hughie, hearing the old man's voice, watching his eyes as he spoke, recognized the sincerity there, and began to realize that he carried an unimaginable responsibility on his shoulders.

On the fourth and fifth days out, there was little to do and Hughie amused both of them by reading aloud, at Nudnick's insistence, from some of his store of books and magazines. At first Hughie was diffident; he could not believe that Nudnick, who had so outdone any fictional scientist, could be genuinely interested; but Nudnick put it as an order, and Hughie began to read, with many a glance at the old man to see if he could find the first glimmerings of derision. He found difficulty in controlling his voice and his saliva until Nudnick slowed him down. Soon he was lost in the yarn. It was a good one.

It concerned one Satan Strong, Scientist, Scourge of the Spaceways and Supporter of the Serialized Short-story. Satan was a bad egg whose criminality was surpassed only by his forte for Science on the Spot. Pursued particularly by the Earth sections of the Space Patrol, Satan Strong was always succeeding in the most dastardly deeds, which always turned out to be the preliminaries to greater evils which were always thwarted by the quick thinking of Captain Jaundess of the Patrol, following which, by "turning to the micro-ultra-philtmeter he rapidly tore out a dozen connections, spot-welded twenty-seven busbars, and converted the machine into an improved von Krockmeier hyperspace lever, which bent space like the blade of a rapier and hurtled him in a flash from hilt to point" and effected his escape until the next issue. Nudnick was entranced.

"It's pseudoscience," he chuckled. "I might even say that it's pseudological pseudoscience. But, it's lovely!" He regarded his withered frame quizzically. "Pity I don't have muscles and a widow's peak," he said. "I've got the science but I rather fear I lack glamour. Have you the next issue?"

Hughie had.

Then, on the sixth day, Hughie's reading was interrupted by a shrill whine from the forward instrument panel. A light flashed under a screen; Nudnick walked over to it and flipped a switch. The screen glowed, showing the blackness of space and its crystal points of light. He turned a knob; the points of light swung slowly across the screen until the tiny black ring of the juncture of the crosshairs encircled a slightly luminous spot.

"What is it?" Hughie asked, regretfully laying down his book.

"Company," said Nudnick tersely. "No telling who it is at this distance, unless they want to tell us about themselves by ultraradio. They're on our course, and overtaking."

Hughie stared into the screen. "You had this stern detector running all the time, didn't you? Gee—You don't think it's a pirate, do you?" There was something hopeful in Hughie's tone. Nudnick laughed.

"You want to see science in action, don't you? Heh. I'm afraid I'm going to be a disappointment to you, youngster. We can't travel any faster than we are going now, and that ship quite obviously can."

Hughie flushed. "Well, professor, if you think it's all right—"

Nudnick shook his head. "I don't think it's all right," he said. "Now that we have established that fact, let's get back to your story. To think that Captain Jaundess would be careless enough to let his betrothed get into the clutches of that evil fellow! What will he do to her?"

"But, Professor Nudnick—"

Nudnick took Hughie's arm and steered him across the control room to his chair. "My dear, overanxious young crew, the ship that is pursuing us presents no problem until it overtakes us. That will be in forty-eight hours. In the meantime, Captain Jaundess' girl friend is in far greater danger than we are. Pray proceed."

Most unwillingly, Hughie read on.

Forty-eight hours later, the brisk crackle of an ultraradio ordered them to stand by to be boarded in the name of the Joint Patrol. The destroyer pulled alongside, and a lifeboat carried a slim, strong cable around the *Stoutfella* and, through the mooring eyes, back to the Patrol ship. The cable was used because magnetic grapples are useless on a Nudnick Metal hull. A winch drew the craft together, and a "wind tunnel" boarding stage groped against the outside of the *Stoutfella's* air lock.

"What are you going to do?" asked Hughie desperately.

"We are going to say as little as possible," said Nudnick meaningly, "and we are going to let them in, of course." He actuated the air-lock controls; the boarding stage was hermetically sealed to their hull as the outer and inner doors slid back.

A purple-uniformed Martian yeoman stepped down into the room, followed by his equally ranking shipmate from Earth. The Martian swore and shut his nostril flaps on the sides of his stringy neck with an unpleasant click. "This air is saturated," he squeaked. "You might have had the courtesy to dehydrate it."

"What?" grinned the Earth Patrolman. "And deprive me of the only breath of decent air I've had in nineteen days?" He drew a grateful breath, letting the moisture sink into his half-parched lungs.

The air in Patrol ships was always, since there was no happy medium, too dry for Earthlings and too humid for Martians; for the Martians, living for countless generations on a water-starved planet had developed a water-hoarding metabolism which had never evolved a use for a water surplus.

"Who is in command?" piped the Martian. Nudnick gestured; the Martian immediately turned his back on Hughie. "We have orders from headquarters that this ship is to be searched and disarmed according to Section 398 of the Earth-Mars Code."

"Suspicion of piracy," supplemented the Earthman.

"Piracy?" shouted Hughie, his resentment at last breaking through. "Piracy? Who do you think you are? What do you mean by—"

Three tiny eyes in the back of the Martian's head flipped open. "Has this unpleasantly noisy infant a function?" he demanded, fingering the blaster at his hip.

"He's my crew. Be quiet, Hughie."

"Yeah—take it easy, kiddo," said the Earthman, not unkindly. "Orders are orders in this outfit. You got no fight with us. We just work here."

"Let them alone, Hughie," chimed in Nudnick. "We've little enough armament and they're welcome to it. They have every right." While the Martian stalked out, the scientist turned to the other Patrolman. "This is a Patrol Council order?"

"Of course."

"Who signed it?"

"Councilman Emil Bjornsen."

"Bjornsen? The new member? How has he the right?"

"Council regulations. 'If any matter should be put to a vote, the resulting decision shall be executed in the name of the president of the council, except in such cases where the decision is carried by one vote, when the order shall be executed in the name of the councilman whose vote carried the measure.' Bjornsen, as the most recently appointed councilman, has the last vote. In this case the action was deadlocked and his vote carried it."

"I see. Thank you. I suppose you can't tell me who proposed this order?"

"Sorry."

The Patrolman moved swiftly about the room, covering every inch of space. In spite of his resentment, Hughie had to admire the man's efficiency. The kid stood sullenly against the bulkhead; when the man came to him, he ran his hands quickly over the boy, and with the skill of a practiced "dip," extracted a low-powered pellet-gun from Hughie's side pocket. "You won't want this," he said. "It won't kill anything but cockroaches, and they're too easily fumigated." Glancing around swiftly to see if the Martian had returned from the storerooms yet, he clapped his hand over Hughie's mouth and whispered something. When the Martian came back, the Patrolman was finishing up on the other side of the room, and Hughie was staring at him with an affectionately resentfull wonderment.

"Hardly a thing," complained the Martian shrilly, displaying a sparse armload of side arms and one neuro ray bow chaser. "Never heard of a Martian councilman sending a destroyer after a couple of nitwits on a pleasure cruise."

They saluted and left. In two minutes the ships drifted apart; in five, the destroyer was nothing but a memory and a dwindling spot on the stern visiscreen. Nudnick smiled at Hughie.

"*Tsk*! You certainly flew off the handle, Hughie. When that fellow took away your peashooter, I thought you were going to bite him."

"Nah," said Hughie embarrassed. "He was O.K. I guess I didn't want the gun much anyhow."

There was a silence, while Nudnick inspected the inner air-lock gate and then the air-pressure indicator. Finally Nudnick asked:

"Well, aren't you going to tell me?"

"What?"

"What it was that the Patrolman whispered in your

ear. Or are you going to save it for a climax in the best science-fiction tradition?"

Hughie was saving it for just that. "You don't miss much do you?" he said. "It wasn't nothing much. He said, 'There's a lousy little Martian private ship on your tail. Probably will stay on our spot on your visiscreen for a few days and be on top of you before you know it. Better watch him.' "

"Hm-m-m." Nudnick stared at the screen. "Anything else?" He spoke as if he knew damn well there was something else. Hughie blushed, robbed of the choicest part of his secret.

"Only just that Bjornsen's aboard."

"That still isn't all." Nudnick approached the boy, absolutely dead pan.

"Honest," stammered Hughie, wide-eyed.

Nudnick shook his head, put his hand in his pocket, gave something to Hughie. "There's just this," he said. "He slipped it into my pocket on the way out, just as easily as he slipped it out of yours."

Hughie stared at the gun in his hand with a delight approaching tears.

"A very efficient young man," said Nudnick. "You will notice that he unloaded it."

Three weeks later Professor Nudnick took it upon himself to disconnect the stern visiscreen because Hughie could not pry himself loose from it. The Patrolman had been right; the destroyer had dwindled there until it reached a .008 intensity and then had stayed right there for several days, after which it had grown again until the boy could make out the ship itself. It was no longer the destroyer, it was a plump-lined wicked little Martian sportster. He knew without asking that the little ship was fast and maneuverable beyond all comparison with the *Stoutfella.* It annoyed him almost as much as Nudnick's calm acceptance of the fact that they were being followed, and that there was every possibility of their never returning to Earth, to say nothing of locating and claiming the prosydium aster-

TWO PERCENT INSPIRATION / 147

oid. He took the trouble to say as much. Nudnick
merely raised his eyebrows to uncover his logic and
said:

"Don't go off half-cocked, younker. Granted, the
Martian is following us. I was apparently right about
Bjornsen's hunch; he knows that I have been looking
all over the System for prosydium and that it is rather
unusual for me to go sailing off personally into space.
Ergo, I must have found some. But he doesn't want
me, or you. All he wants is the prosydium. He can get it
only by following this ship. Until we tie on to something, we're as safe as a babe in a bassinet. So why
worry?"

"Why worry?" The kid's brains almost crackled audibly in their attempt to transmit his worry to the scientist. "Here's something! Has it occurred to you that all
the Martian has to do is to determine our course, continue it ahead on a chart, and then know our destination?"

"It has occurred to me," said Nudnick gently. "Our
course will intercept Mercury in twenty days."

"Mercury!" Hughie cried. "You told me the prosydium was on an asteroid!"

"It is on an asteroid." Nudnick was being assiduously
patient. "You know it, and I know it. But our course is
for Mercury. That's all *they* know. If we lose them, we
will change course for the Belt. If we don't lose them,
we will go to Mercury. If they're persistent, we'll go
back to Earth and try again some time, though I will
admit that there's only a billion to one chance of our
slipping away without being followed again."

"I'm sorry," said Hughie after a while. "I have no
business in trying to tell you off, Professor Nudnick.
Only I hate like hell to see that Bjornsen guy keep you
away from what you want to get. That heel. That lousy
wart on the nose of progress!"

"End quotes," said Nudnick dryly. "Captain Jaundess."

"O.K., O.K.," said Hughie, grinning in spite of himself. "But I can't seem to get over that guy Bjornsen.

He got in my hair for nearly two years at school, and now that he's kicked me out he seems to want to get under my scalp as well. I dunno—I never saw a guy like that before. I can't figger him—the way he thinks. That rotten business of ganging up on kids. He's inhuman!"

"You may be right," said Nudnick slowly. "You may just possibly be right." After a long pause, he said, "I picked the right assistant, Hughie, You're doing fine."

Hughie was so tickled by that remark that he didn't think to ask what provoked it.

Two days before they were due on Mercury, the professor heaved a sigh, glanced at Hughie, and connected up the stern visiscreen. "There you are," he said quietly. Hughie looked up from his magazine, dropped it with a gasp of horror. The Martian ship was not two hundred yards behind them, looming up, filling the screen. He sprang to his feet.

"Professor Nudnick! *Do* something!"

Nudnick shook his head, spread his hands. "Any ideas?"

"There must be something. Can't you blast them, professor?"

"With what? The Patrol took even our little neuro ray."

Hughie waved the defeatist philosophy aside impatiently. "There ought to be something you could do. Heck—you're supposed to be ten times the scientist that Harry Petrou is—"

"I beg your pardon?"

"Harry Petrou ... Petrou!" Hughie swept up the magazine, thrust the too-bright cover in the scientist's face. "The writer! The author of—"

"Satan Strong!" The dried-up old man let out an astonishingly hearty peal of laughter.

"Well," said Hughie defensively, "anyway—" Furiously he began to shout half hysterical phrases. He was scared, and he had a bad case of hero worship, and he was also very young. He said, "You go ahead and laugh. But Harry Petrou has some pretty damn good ideas. Maybe they're not scientific. Not what you'd call scientific. Why doesn't anybody ever do anything scientific without studying for fifty years in a dusty old laboratory? Why does one of the greatest scientists in history," he half sobbed, "sit back and b-be bullied by a l-louse like Bjornsen?"

"Hughie—take it easy, there." Nudnick put out his hand, then turned away from those young, accusing eyes. "Things aren't done that way, Hughie. Science isn't like that—made to order for melodramatic adventures. I know—you'd like me to burrow into the air conditioner, throw a few connections around, and come out with a space-warp."

Hughie turned on the lower forward screen. It showed, blindingly, the flaming crescent of the inner planet. They were descending swiftly toward the night-edge of the twilight strip, the automatic pilot taking care of every detail of deceleration and gravity control.

"You're quitting," said Hughie, his lip quivering. "You're running away!" And he turned his back to Nudnick, to stare at the evil menacing bulk of the Martian ship.

Nudnick sighed, went and sat at the controls, and took over the ship from the pilot.

After two silent hours, Hughie observed that Nudnick was preparing to land. He said, in a dead voice:

"If you land, they'll catch us."

"That's right." Nudnick's voice was brisk.

"And if they catch us, they'll torture us."

"Yep." Nudnick glanced over his shoulder. "Will you obey my orders implicitly?"

"Sure," said Hughie hopelessly. His eyes were fixed in fearful fascination on the Martian ship.

"Start now, then. Get rid of all the metal on your clothes. Belt buckle, buttons—everything. You have fiber soled boots?"

"Mm-m-m."

"Put them on. Snap into it!"

An hour later the *Stoutfella* grated on a sandy clearing not far from a red and rocky bluff. The choking atmosphere of Mercury swirled about the portholes. Nudnick climbed out of the pilot seat and tore a pair of fiber boots out of a locker. He had already ripped his buttons off, tossed his wrist radio and identification ring on the chart table. "Come on!" he snapped.

"You . . . we're not going out there?"

"You're damn right we are."

Hughie looked at him. If this old man was willing—He shrugged, picked up a magazine. It seemed as if he—stroked it. Then he. tossed it aside and strode with Nudnick into the air lock.

As the inner gate shut them out of the little world that the ship afforded, Nudnick clapped him on the back. "Chin up, kiddo," he said warmly. "Now listen—do exactly as I tell you. When we get outside, move as fast as you can toward that bluff. The Martians won't shoot as long as they think we have any information. Na—no questions—there isn't time! Listen. It's hot out there. As hot as the oven my dear old mother used to bake ten-egg cakes in. The air is not so good, but we can breathe it—for a while. Long enough, I guess. Ready?"

The outer gate slid back and they plunged out.

It was hot. In seconds acrid dust was packing on Hughie's skin, washing away in veritable gushes of sweat, packing the pores again. He saw the reason for taking off metal clothing. He had left his identification ring on; it began to sear his hand. He tore it off, and blistered flesh with it.

The air lacerated his throat, stung his eyes. Somehow he knew the location of three things—the red bluff, the hovering Martian ship, and the professor. He pounded on. Once he tripped, went down on one knee. His breeches burst into flame. Nudnick saw and helped him slap it out. Inside the charred edges of cloth he caught a glimpse of his own kneecap, a tiny spot of bone amid a circle of cooked flesh, where his knee had ground into the burning sand.

Nudnick tugged at his elbow. "How far do you think we are?" he wheezed.

Hughie suddenly realized that Nudnick's old eyes couldn't see very far in this kind of heat; he had to be eyes for two people now. "Ship—hundred and fifty —yards—"

"Not—far enough! Go—on!"

They struggled on, helping each other, hindering each other. The ground rose sharply; Nudnick stopped. "Beginning of ... bluff ... far ... enough—" He began coughing.

Hughie held him up until he had finished. He began to understand. He had heard vague stories about Martian torture. Nudnick would rather die this way, then. They could have starved slowly in the ship. Maybe this was better—

Nudnick's shrill, dust-choked whisper reached him. "Martians?"

Hughie put one hand over his eyes and peered through the fingers. The Martian ship had settled down beside the *Stoutfella*. The port swung open, three figures, two tall and lanky, one short and shriveled. "Three ... coming ... two Martians ... Bjornsen." Talking was torture. Breathing was pulling living fire into the lungs. He heard a noise and looked down. Nudnick was clutching him and making the noise. Slowly he realized that the old man was laughing.

They lurched toward the three figures, clinging to each other. The two Martians grasped them, and just in time, or they would have fallen and died.

"Of all the crazy damn things to do!" shrilled Bjornsen. In spite of the blazing breeze, the insufferable heat, the old gestures returned to him, and he rubbed his hands together in that familiar, despised gesture.

Nudnick forced his eyes open and stared at the councilman worriedly, and then turned to each of the Martians. They were wilting a little bit in the heat, but their grip was still strong. Bjornsen spoke a few squeaky words in the Martian tongue, and the five of them began to struggle toward the ships.

Suddenly the Martian who had Hughie's arm began to cry out in a piercing, undulating whine. It was quite the most ghastly sound the boy had ever heard; he shuddered in spite of the heat and thrust at the creature. To his utter amazement the Martian slumped to the ground, arched his back as it began to scorch, screamed deafeningly and then lay still. Nudnick laughed cacklingly again and shoved at his Martian, tripping him at the same time. The second Martian stumbled, regained his balance, and then began screaming. In a matter of seconds he fell. He took longer, but died also—

Bjornsen stood in front of them, watching the Martians, and then, shouting agonized curses, began a stumbling run toward his ship.

"Damn it, he's going to make it!" cried Nudnick; and stooping, he caught up a hot stone and hurled it.

Straight as an explosive pellet it flew, and caught Bjornsen between his narrow shoulders. Bjornsen threw up his hands, trying wildly to keep his feet. Gibbering crazily, Nudnick threw another stone. It missed by twenty feet. Hughie caught the old man as he fell exhausted. When next he looked at Bjornsen, the councilman was down on his knees, his hand clutching at the sill of the Martian's air lock. He sagged, writhed, and died there.

Hughie stood for five seconds, tottering; then he shook his head, bent and let the scientist's limp body fall across his shoulder. It took him an eternity to straighten up, and then eternities to locate his nearby ship and begin that long, long, fifty-foot journey. Hughie knew later that if it had been five—three—feet more, he could not possibly have made it. But somehow he did—somehow he tumbled the old man into the lock, pitched forward on top of him. He scrabbled weakly around, found the lock control, pressed it.

Hughie screamed when he came out of it. Then he opened his eyes and saw that he wasn't in that fiery desert. He closed them again and realized that his knee hurt terribly. Then Nudnick was beside him, bathing his face, talking.

"Good stuff, kid. Fix you up in no time. Heh! Long chance just for a few tons of prosydium, eh? Well, we'll get it now. No one else around. No one else around."

"Bjornsen?"

"Dead. Remember? Like the Martians."

"Martians." The words brought horror into the heat-reddened young face. He raised his head and Nudnick slipped another pillow under it. "What happened to those Martians?"

Nudnick grinned. "They died of ignorance, son, and let that be a lesson to you." Hughie just stared. "You see, for generations now, Martians have lived on Earth and Earthmen on Mars. It made 'em forget something—that one little fact I was talking about before we landed. Water-hoarders, Hughie. *Martians can't sweat!* You see? A human can live beside a steak that's cooking, because he sweats. The evaporation cools him down. A Martian can't stand that kind of heat—he cooks like a steak!"

"But . . . Bjornsen wasn't—"

"Ah. You're wrong there. Bjornsen *was!* A freak, Hughie. Look at Martians. Unemotional—logical—well, isn't that Bjornsen? Y'know, when I walked in on him when he was ganging up on you at the Institute, I heard him rub his hands together. I knew I'd heard it somewhere before, but I didn't know just where. But the other day when you said he was inhuman, it clicked. Bjornsen didn't have no mamma and no poppa, kiddo. He came out of a Martian biochemical laboratory, or I miss my guess. Clever fellers, those Martians. Trained him from birth for that job. A key man in the middle of my little old institute, There may be more like him. I'll see to that. Heh! I won't be the first boss that's told his employees, 'Work up a sweat or get canned!' "

Hughie at last managed to grin a little. Nudnick kept on talking happily. "The knee'll be all right in a couple weeks. By that time we'll hook on to the prosydium.

You're fixed for life, fella. Ah—hey, I've got a confession to make to you."

Hughie turned weak, amused eyes on him. The old man wagged his head. "Yep. About that prosydium. Didn't you wonder how I knew about it? I'll tell you. I was coming from Mars last year on a Martian liner. Very elegant. Humidifiers in every room. Radio. Recorded music. Lots of apparatus built into the staterooms. Would've delighted the heart of Satan Strong. Anyway, I got messing around. I . . . er—" He paused guiltily, then went on. "I sort of tore out some connections and spot-welded some busbars. Built me a dandy little detectograph. Located that prosydium as we passed the edge of the Belt. Sheer luck. Spotted it, by golly, right from a stateroom in a Martian ship!"

Hughie laughed admiringly. "You old son of a gun," he said disrespectfully. "And you sneered at Satan Strong!"

"Me?" The old man shook his head and stood up. "Why should I sneer at Satan Strong? I *like* Satan Strong. I ought to. I *write* those stories!"

The story of the origin of CARGO will gladden the heart of the string-saver—in fact, the tale might well have been called "Salvage." In the first draft of another story (THE ULTIMATE EGOIST), the protagonist at one point debated the advisability of going to sea. In the first draft of that tale, he actually did, and for some three thousand words found himself on a tanker on which weird things happened. I realized suddenly that I was getting far away from my story, and cut back. But instead of throwing away these extraneous pages, I saved them and expanded them: CARGO is the result.

Cargo

I heard somebody say she was haunted. She wasn't haunted. There's another name for what ailed her, and I'll tell you about if you like. I was aboard her when it started, and before. I knew every sheared rivet on her. I knew her when she was honest, a drab and prosaic member of our merchant marine. I saw what happened to her.

She was one of those broad-shouldered old hulks built by the dozen during War I. Her sisters lay rotting and rusting and waiting for a national emergency to prove their unseaworthiness. O.K. They make good shrapnel. Her name was *Dawnlight,* she was seven thousand tons, a black oil tanker, limped like a three-legged dog, and was as beautiful as a wart. She could do nine knots downhill with a fair wind and an impossible current. When she was loaded she steered well until the loss of weight from burned fuel in the after bunkers threw her down by the head, and then she proceeded as will any tanker with a loss back aft; when she was light she drew seventeen feet aft and nothing forward, so that when the wind blew abeam she spun on her tail like a canoe.

Yes, I knew her of old. She used to carry casinghead. That's airplane gas that makes explosive vapors at around 40°F. So one day a fireman found casinghead seeping through the seams of No. 9 tank into the fireroom and evaporating there. He fainted dead away, and the crew took to the boats during the night. The Old Man woke up at noon the next day screaming for his coffee, put two and two together, and with the help of two engineers and a messman, worked her into a cove in a small island off Cuba.

It so happened that a very wealthy gentleman thereabouts turned up a nice offer, with the result that the Old Man and his three finks made for Havana in a lifeboat with their pockets full of large bills and the ship's log, which contained an entry describing her explosion and sinking. After that she carried crude oil for the wealthy gentleman to war zones. Great sport.

What made it such great sport was that not only did the *Dawnlight* have no business being afloat, but she had no business being in her particular business. Her nationality was determined by the contents of the flag locker, and her current log looked like a set of the Encyclopædia Britannica. They'd run up one flag or another, and pick a log to suit.

But she paid well and she fed well, and if you could keep away from the ocean floor and the concentration camps, you'd find her good shipping. If you must commit suicide, you might as well get rich doing it.

I caught her in a certain drydock that makes a good thing out of doing quick work and asking few questions. Her skipper was a leathery old squarehead whose viscera must have been a little brown jug. Salt cracked off his joints when he moved. He was all man back aft and all devil on the bridge, and he owned our souls. Not that that was much of a possession. The crew matched the ship, and they were the crummiest, crustiest, hardbitten bunch of has-been human beings ever to bless the land by going to sea. Had to be that way.

Any tanker is a five-hundred-foot stick of dynamite, even if she isn't an outlaw. If she's loaded, she'll burn forever and a week; and if she's light she'll go sky-high and never come down. All she needs is a spark from somewhere. That can happen easily enough any time; but imagine dodging subs and pocket battleships on both sides of the martial fence—swift, deadly backstabbers, carrying many and many a spark for our cargoes. We had nothing for protection but luck and the Old Man. We stuck to him.

The *Dawnlight* was the only ship I'd have taken, feeling the way I was. Once in a while the world gangs up on a guy, and he wants an out. The *Dawnlight* was mine—she'd pulled me through a couple of dark spots in the past—once when a certain dope fell and cracked his silly skull in a brawl over a girl, and I had to disappear for a while, and once when I married the girl and she took to blackmailing me for a living. Aside from all this, though, the *Dawnlight* was the only ship I *could* get aboard. I carried an ordinary seaman's certificate, endorsed for wiper. The Department of Commerce was very lenient with me and let me keep those ratings after I ran a naval auxiliary tanker on the rocks. Passed out drunk on watch. Anyhow, the Old Man gave me the eight-to-twelve watch as third mate, papers or no papers. It was that kind of a ship. He was that kind of a skipper. He had the idea I was that kind of a sailor.

We left the drydock (it's up North somewhere—that'll do!) and headed east and south. We were in ballast, carrying only two hundred big cases of farm machinery in the two dry cargo holds. Farm machinery with steel-jacketed noses and percussion caps. Nice chunky crates of tractors with rifled barrels. We followed the coastline pretty much, but stayed far off, out of the southbound steamer lanes. This wasn't long after the beginning of the war, when all hands ashore and afloat were excited about neutrality zones, so we wanted to keep our noses clean. However, we weren't

too worried. We weren't the only gray-painted, uniden-
tified hulk at sea by any means, and anyway, we had
the skipper.

We dropped down to about 33° and headed due
east. It was early fall—the hurricane season—but the
weather was fine and mellow. We kept the morning sun
a point off the starboard bow, and in the evening we
tore up the base of the shadow we threw ahead. The
black gang talked of an unheard-of sixty-three revolu-
tions per minute from the engine, when she hadn't done
better than fifty-seven in the last twelve years. Every
time I shot the sun or a star on my watch, the ship
stood still and waited for me to get it, and I navigated
as if I had a radio beam in my pocket. It didn't seem
like the old *Dawnlight* any more, with her rotten gear
and her chewing-gum calking. It was a pleasure to
work her. Even Cajun Joe's sea bread stopped giving
me heartburn.

Yes, it was too good to be true, so in the long run it
didn't turn out to be true. After we reached longtitude
30° everything about that ship went haywire. Nothing
was really wrong, only—well, there was the matter of
the sextants, for instance. Four of them—mine, and the
first's, and the second's, but worst of all, the Old Man's
ancient binocular-type monster. They all went just a little bit off—enough to throw us eight or ten degrees off
course. You see, after we passed 30, we changed course
a shade north to head us up toward Gibraltar; and no
sooner had we done that than clouds popped up from
nowhere and the weather got really thick.

Nights we sailed in a black soup, and days we sailed
in a white one, and the compass was the only thing that
would even admit where we might be. Things got
screwy. The revolution counter said we were making a
wabbly seven point two knots. The patent log claimed
an even six. But it wasn't until the third day of fog,
about five bells on my morning watch, that we really
found out that we were being led astray. About the sextants, I mean.

There was a hole in the clouds, high on the starboard beam; I saw it coming up, figured it would show the sun, and whistled up the Old Man and the mate. I was right; it was a small hole, and as the three of us lined up on the wing of the bridge with our sextants, the second came bumbling sleepily up with his. Old Johnny Weiss was at the wheel, steadying the lubber-line onto the compass card the only way an old shellback trained in sail can steer a ship.

"Watch the clock, Johnny," I said and got the image of that cloud hole on my mirror.

"Hi," he said, which was the nearest any of us came to "Aye-aye, sir," on that scow.

We froze there, the four of us, each sextant steady as a rock, waiting for the gleam. It came, and the Old Man said "Hup!" and we fixed our arcs.

We got the time from Johnny—the old clock in the wheelhouse was chronometer enough for us—and we broke out our tables. Our four sights came out close enough. Position, 31° 17′ N, 33° 9′ 40″ W—which landed us about four hundred miles due east of the Madeiras. We found that if we split the difference between the distance-run given by the deck and engine logs, we'd reach that position by dead reckoning. It looked good—too good. The *Dawnlight* was balky steering, what with her outmoded hydraulic telemotor and her screw-type steering engine. She'd never performed that way.

As soon as I was alone in the chart house I went over my figures. Everything was jake, but—the primary mirror on my sextant was askew. Slipped down a bit in its frame. Why, a thing like that could prove us a hundred and fifty miles off course! It had never happened before—it was a new sextant, and I took care of it. Now how in—

I slipped down to the Old Man's office and went in. He and the mate were bent over the desk. They straightened as I came in.

"Cap'n, I—"

"Vot reading dit you get on your sun gun?" he asked

me before I could finish my speech. I told him. He scratched his head and looked at the mate.

The mate said: "Yeah, me, too." He was a Boston Irishman named Toole; four foot eleven in his shoes. He was wanted for four very elaborate murders, He collected seventeenth-century miniatures. "I got the same thing, only my sextant's on the bum. That couldn't be right. Look—the eyepiece on the 'scope is off center."

"Look now here," The Old Man took down his behemoth, and showed me a gradation plate sliding around loosely over its pulled rivets. "Yust py accident I gat the same."

"My gosh! That's what I came down to tell you, skipper. Look at this." I showed him the loose mirror on my instrument.

Just then Harry, the second mate, edged into the room. He always edged through doors on the mistaken assumption that he was thinner fore and aft than he was across the beam. It was hard to tell. Harry saw everything and said nothing, and if he was as innocent as he hugely looked, he would not have been aboard the *Dawnlight*. He said:

"Cap, m' readin' on that sight was off. My sextant—"

"—has gone gebrochen. Don't tell me dis too."

"Why . . . yeh. Yeh."

"Four sextants go exactly the same amount off at the same time for four different reasons," said Toole, examining a bent arc track on Harry's sun gun. The captain sighed.

No one said anything for a minute, and we hardly noticed it when the captain's deck lamp winked off. The engine room speaking tube shrieked and I answered it because I was nearest. I heard:

"Skipper?"

"Third mate."

"Tell the Old Man that No. 2 generator just threw its armature. Cracked the casing all to hell."

"What's the matter with No. 1?"

"Damfino. Fused solid two hours ago. And no spares for anything, and no cable to wind a new armature."

"O.K." I turned and told the skipper.

He almost laughed. "I vas yust going to say dot ve'd haf to take a radio bearing on Gibraltor and Feisal. Heh. Didn't y'u tell me, 'Arry, dot dere vas no acid for the batteries on the radio?"

"I did."

"Heh." The skipper drummed for a moment on his desk, looking at me without seeing me. Then he saw me. "Vot de dirty hell are y'u duing down here ven y'u're on vatch? Gat up dere!"

I got—there were times when you couldn't play around with the old boy.

Up on deck the weather looked the same. The sea was slick and the air was warm, and I had to fumble around to locate the bridge ladder. Johnny was steering steadily, easily, a couple of spokes each way every couple of minutes. He was the only man aboard that had the feel of that crazy ship, with her warped keel and her scored and twisted propeller. He looked up at me as I stepped into the wheelhouse and grunted.

"What's up, Johnny?"

"Reckon you know where we are, huh?"

"I reckon."

No sense in getting the crew talking. Sailors gossip like a bridge club, and for the same reason—grouped people with the same basic interests. I've seen three quarters of a crew packed up and ready to leave because some wiseacre started the rumor that a ship was going to be sold for scrap at the next port.

Johnny grunted, and I went into the chart room to monkey with that slipped glass in my sextant. The way the weather looked, I'd never have a chance to use it again, but then you can't tell about an African coastwise fog. What had made Johnny so quizzical? The more I tried to think of something else, the more that bothered me. About ten minutes later, working on the theory that the last word said before a long pause is the one that sticks, I went back into the wheelhouse and asked:

"Why do you want to know?"

"Oh, nothing'." He spat, and the tobacco juice rang a knell on the cuspidor. "Jest thinkin'."

"Come on—give."

"Waal—seems to me we been steerin' east b' nor'east about two days—right?"

"So?"

"Youse guys was so busy peekin' through yer sextants at the Big Light that you didn't see it was in the wrong place."

"The sun? In the wrong place?"

"Yep. Steerin' east b' nor'east this time o' year, hereabouts, seems to me the sun'd show about broad on the bow at ten thirty in th' mornin'."

"Well?"

"So it shows up high an' dead abeam. Don't seem right, somehow."

He was right. I went and sat down on the pilot's stool. Radio dead, sextants haywire; all we have is the compass and good old Bowditch's dead-reckoning tables. And now—the compass?

"Johnny, are you sure you were on course when we took that sight?"

His silence was eloquent. Old Johnny Weiss could steer anything with a rudder unless it had a steering oar, and then he was better than most. If we had a radio, we could check the compass. We had no radio. If we could get a sun sight, we wouldn't need the radio. We couldn't get a sun sight. We were lost—lost as hell. We were steering a rock-steady compass course on a ship that was pounding the miles away under her counter as she had never done before, and she was heading bravely into nowhere.

An ordinary seaman popped in. "Lost the patent log, sir!"

Before I could say, "Oh, well, it didn't work, anyway," the engine-room tube piped up.

"Well?" I said into it, in the tone that means "Now what?"

It was the third engineer again. "Is the skipper up there?"

"No. What is it?"

"A lot of things happen," wailed the third. "Why do they all have to happen to *me?*"

"You don't know, shipmate, you don't know! What's up?"

"The rev-counter arm worked loose and fell into the crank pit. The I.P. piston grabbed it and hauled counter and all in. Goddlemighty, what goes on here? We jinxed?"

"Seems as though," I said, and whistled down the captain's tube to report the latest.

Everything depended on our getting a sun sight now. We might have calculated our speed at least from the revolution readings, a tide chart and propslip table. The admiralty charts don't give a damn about this particular section of sea water. Why should they? There's supposed to be a deep around the Madeiras somewhere, but then again there's flat sand aplenty off Africa. Even the skipper's luck wouldn't pull us out of this. I had a feeling. Damn it, we couldn't even hail a ship, if we met one. It would be bound to turn out a q-ship or a sub-chaser, tickled to death to pinch our cargo. Farm machinery. Phooey!

The saloon messman came up carrying clean sheets for the chart-room cot. I knew what that meant. The bridge was going to be the skipper's little home until we got out of this—if we did. I was dead beat. Things like this couldn't happen—they *couldn't!*

We had a council of war that night, right after I came on watch, the captain and I. Nothing had happened all day; the sun came out only once, on the twelve to four, and ducked in again so quickly that Harry couldn't get to his sextant. He did set the pelorus on it, but the ship rolled violently because of some freak current just as he sighted, and the altitude he got was all off. There'd been nothing else—Oh, yes; we'd lost three heaving lines over the side, trying to gauge our speed with a chip. The darnedest thing about it was that everything else was going as well as it possibly could.

The cook had found nine crates of really fancy canned goods in the linen locker—Lord knows how long they'd been there. It was just as if they'd been dropped out of nowhere. The engines ran without a hitch. The low-pressure cylinder lost its wheeze, and in the washrooms we got hot water when we wanted it instead of cold water or steam. Even the mattresses seemed softer. Only we just didn't know where we were.

The Old Man put his hand on my shoulder and startled me, coming up behind me in the darkness that way. I was standing out on the wing of the bridge.

"Vot's de matter; vorried about de veather?" he asked me. He was funny that way, keeping us on our toes with his furies and his—what was it?—kindnesses.

"Well, yes, cap'n, I don't like the looks of this."

He put his elbows on the coaming. "I tell y'u boy, ve ain't got nodding to fret about."

"Oh, I guess not, but I don't go for this hide-'n'-go-seek business." I could feel him regarding me carefully out of the corners of his eyes.

"I vant to tell y'u something. If I said dis to de mate, or Harry, or vun or de black gang, dev vould say: 'I t'ink de ol' squarehead is suckin' vind. He must be gettin' old.' But I tell y'u."

I was flattered.

"Dis is a old ship but she is good. I am going to be sorry to turn her over to sumvun else."

"What are you talking about, skipper? You're not quitting when we get back?"

"No; before dat. Dass all I vorry about, y'u see. Dis vill be de first command I lost half a trip out. I vass master of thirty-two ships, but I alvays left dem in der home port. It von't be like dat now."

I was more than a little taken aback. I'd never seen

the stringy old gun runner sentimental about his ship before. This was the first time I'd ever heard him mention it in printable terms. But what was all this about losing his command?

"What's the matter, cap'n—think we'll go to camp?" That was a *Dawnlight* idiom and meant being picked up by a warship of some kind.

"No boy—nodding like dat. Dey can't touch us. Nobody can touch us now. Ah—hear dat?"

He pointed far out to port. The night was very still, with hardly a sound but the continual seethe of millions of bursting bubbles slithering past the ship's side. But far out in the fog was an insistent splashing—that heavy smacking splash that every seaman knows.

"Porpoise," I said.

The skipper tugged at my elbow and led me through the wheelhouse to the other wing. "Listen."

There it was again, on the starboard side. "Must be quite a few of 'em," I said laconically, a little annoyed that he should change the subject that way.

"Dere is plenty, but dey are not porpoises."

"Blackfish?"

"Dey is not fish, too. Dey is somet'ing y'u have seen in books. Dey is vimmin with tails on."

"What?"

"O.K., I vas kidding. Call me ven y'u are relieved."

In the green glow from the starboard running light I saw him hand me a piercing gaze; then he shambled back to the chart room. A little bit short of breath, I went into the wheelhouse and lit a cigarette.

The cuspidor rang out, and I waited for Johnny to speak.

"The skipper ain't nuts," he said casually.

"Somebody is," I returned. "You heard him, then."

"Listen—if the skipper told me the devil himself was firing on the twelve to four, then the devil it would be." Johnny was fiercely loyal under that armor of easy talk. "I've heard them 'porpoises' of yours for three days now. Porpoises don't follow a ship two hundred yards off. They'll jump the bow wave fer a few minutes an' then high-tail, or they'll cross yer bow an' play away. These is different. I've gone five degrees off to port an' then to starboard to see if I could draw 'em. Nope; they keep their distance." Johnny curled some shag under his lip.

"Aw, that's . . . that's screwy, Johnny."

He shrugged. "You've shipped with the Old Man before. He sees more than most of us." And that's all he'd say.

It was about two days later that we began to load. Yeah, that's what I said. We didn't dock, and we didn't discharge our farm machinery. We took on—whatever it was our cargo turned out to be. It was on the four to eight in the evening when the white fog was just getting muddy in the dusk. I was dead asleep when the ship sat down on her tail, stuck her bow up and heeled over. The engines stopped, and I got up from the corner of my room where the impact had flung me.

She lay still on her side, and hell was breaking loose. Toole had apparently fallen up against the fire-alarm button, and the lookout forward was panicky and ringing a swing symphony on the bell. A broken steam line was roaring bloody murder, and so was the second mate. The whistle, at least, was quiet—it had fallen with a crash from the "Pat Finnegan" pipe.

I leaned against the wall and crouched into a pair of pants and staggered out on deck. I couldn't see a blasted thing. If the fog had been thick before, it was twenty times as thick now.

Someone ran into me, and we both went skittering into the scuppers. It was the mate on his way down to the captain's room. Why the Old Man wasn't on the bridge, I couldn't savvy, unless it had to do with that peculiar attitude of resignation about his imagined loss of command.

"What the hell?" I wanted to know.

Toole said: "Who is that—third mate? Oh. I don't know. We've hit something. We're right up on top of it. Ain't rocks; didn't hear any plates go. Isn't sand; no sand bank this size could stay this far from land."

"Where's the skipper?"

"In his room, far as I know. C'mon, let's roll him out."

We groped our way to the alleyway door and into the midship house. Light was streaming from the skipper's room, and as we approached the door we heard the rare, drawn-out chuckle. I'll never forget the shock of seeing this best of captains, a man who had never dented a bilge plate in his life, sprawled back in his tilted swivel chair with his feet on a tilted desk, chuckling into a tilted bottle of Scotch.

Toole squawked: "Cap'n! We've struck something!"

The skipper giggled. He had a terrific load on. I leaned past Toole and shook him. "Skipper! We've struck!"

He looked at us blearily. "Heh. Sid-down, boyss, de trip iss over. Ve have not struck. Ve is yust finished. Heh!"

"Clear the boats," Toole said aside to me.

The skipper heard him. "Vait!" he said furiously, and lurched to his feet. "I am still in command here! Don't lower no boats. Ve are not in distress, y'u hear? Heh! Ve are loading. I know all about it. Go an' see for y'uselfs, so y'u don't belief me!"

Toole stared at the captain for a moment. I stood by. If Toole decided the Old Man was nuts, he'd take over. If not, then the squarehead was still running the show. Suddenly Toole leaned over and cut the master switch on the alarm system. It had a separate little battery circuit of its own, and was the only thing electrical aboard that still operated. The silence was deafening as the alarm bells throughout the ship stilled, and we could hear a bumble of voices from back aft as the crew milled about. They were a steady bunch; there would be no panic. Toole beckoned me out of the room and left. Once we were outside he said:

"What do you think?"

"I think he's—I dunno, Toole. He's a seaman first and a human being afterward. If he says we're not in distress, it's likely true. Course, he's drunk."

Toole snorted. "He thinks better when he's drunk. Come on, let's look around."

We dropped down the ladder. The ship lay still. She was careened, probably with her starboard side under water and the starboard rail awash.

Toole said: "Let's go to port. Maybe we can see what it is we've hit."

We had to go on all fours to get up there, so steeply was the deck canted. It did us no good; there was nothing to be seen anywhere but fog.

Toole clung with one arm to the chain rail and puffed, "Can't see a thing down there, can you?"

I hung over the edge. "Can't even see the water line."

"Let's go down to the starboard side. She must be awash there."

She was. I stepped ankle-deep into sea water before I knew where I was. The sea was dead calm, and the fog was a solid thing; and something was holding the ship heeled over. I tell you, it was a nasty feeling. If only we knew what was under us! And then—we saw the ship being loaded.

May I never see another sight like that one. As if to tease and torture us, the fog swirled silently away from the ship's side, leaving a little dim island of visibility for us to peer into. We could see fifty or sixty feet of deck, and the chain rails fore and aft dipping into the sea at our feet; and we could see a round patch of still water with its edges wetting the curtain of fog. And on that patch of water were footprints. We both saw them at the same time and froze, speechless. Coming toward us over the water they were—dozens of them. The water was like a resilient, glossy sheet of paving, and the impression of dozens—hundreds—of feet ran across it to the ship. But there was nothing making the footprints. Just—footprints. Oh, my God!

There were big splay ones and big slow ones, and little swift ones and plodding ones. Once something long and invisible crept with many legs up to the ship, and once little pointed feet, high-arched, tripped soundlessly over the chains and *something* fell sprawling a yard from where we stood. There was no splash, but just the indentation in the water of a tiny, perfect body that rolled and squirmed back onto its feet and ran over to the deck and disappeared. I suddenly felt that I was in the midst of a milling crowd of—of people. Nothing touched me, and yet, all around me was the pressure of scores of beings who jostled each other and pushed and shoved, in their eagerness to get aboard. It was ghastly. There was no menace in it, nor anything to fear except that here was a thing that could not be understood.

The fog closed down suddenly, and for a long moment we stood there, feeling the pressure of that mob of "passengers"; and then I reached out and found the mate's arm and tugged him toward the midship house. We crawled up the canted ladder and stood by the glow from the lamp in the captain's room.

"It's a lot of goddam nonsense," I said weakly.

"Hm-m-m."

I didn't know whether or not Toole agreed with me.

The skipper's voice came loosely from the porthole. "Heh! I cert'n'y t'ank y'u for de Scotch, I du. Vat a deal, vat a deal!" And he burst out into a horrible sound that might have been laughter, in his cracked and grating voice. I stared in. He was nodding and grinning at the forward bulkhead, toasting it with a pony of fire water.

"He's seein' things," said the mate abruptly.

"Maybe all the rest of us are blind," I said; and the mate's dazed expression made me wonder, too, why I had said that. Without another word he went above to take over the bridge, while I went aft to quiet the crew.

We lay there for fourteen hours, and all the while that invisible invasion continued. There was nothing any of us could do. And crazy things began happening. Any one of them might have happened to any of us once in a while, but—well, judge for yourself, now. When I came on watch that night there was nothing to do but stand by, since we were hove to, and I set Johnny to polishing brass. He got his polish and his rag and got to work. I mooned at the fog from the wheelhouse window, and in about ten minutes I heard Johnny cuss and throw a rag and can over the side.

"What gives, Johnny?"

"Ain't no use doin' this job. Must be the fog." He pointed to the binnacle cover. "The tarnish smells the polish and fades off all around me rag. On'y where I rub it comes in stronger."

It was true. All the places he had rubbed were black-green, and around those spots the battered brass gleamed brilliantly! I told John to go have himself a cup of coffee and settled down on the stool to smoke.

No cigarettes in the right pocket of my dungarees. None in the left. I *knew* I'd put a pack there. "Damn!" I muttered. Now where the—what was I looking for? Cigarettes? But I had a pack of cigarettes in my hand! Was I getting old or something? I tried to shrug it off. I must have had them there all the time, only—well, things like that don't happen to me! I'm not absentminded. I pulled out a smoke and stuck it in my chops, fumbling for a match. Now where—I did some more cussing. No matches. What good is a fag to a guy without a—I gagged suddenly on too much smoke. Why was I looking for a match? My cigarette was lit!

When a sailor starts to get the jitters he usually begins to think about the girl he left behind him. It was just my luck to be tied up with one I didn't want to think about. I simply went into a daze while I finished that haunted cigarette. After a while Johnny came back carrying a cup of coffee for me.

Now I like my coffee black. Wet a spoon in it and dip it in the sugar barrel, and that's enough sugar for me. Johnny handed me the cup, and I took the saucer off the rim. The coffee was creamed—on a ship that means evaporated milk—and sweet as a soft caramel.

"Damn it, Johnny, you know how I like my coffee. What's the idea of this?"

"What?"

I showed him. When he saw the pale liquid he recoiled as if there had been a snake curled up on the saucer instead of a cup. "S'help me, third, I didn't put a drop of milk in that cup! Nor sugar, neither!"

I growled and threw cup and saucer over the side. I couldn't say anything to Johnny. I *knew* he was telling the truth. Oh, well, maybe there happened to be some milk and sugar in the cup he used and he didn't notice it. It was a weak sort of excuse, but I clung to it.

At six bells the second heaved himself up the ladder. "O.K.—you're relieved," he said.

"At eleven o'clock? What's the idea?"

"Aw—" His huge bulk pulsed as he panted, and he was sweating. "I couldn't sleep, that's all. Shove off."

"I'll be damned! First time I ever heard of you rolling out before you were called, Harry. What's the matter—this canting too much for you?" The ship still lay over at about 47°.

"Naw. I c'n sleep through twice that. It was—Oh, go below, third."

"O.K. Course 'n' speed the same—zero-zero. The wind is on the weather side, an' we're runnin' between the anchors. The bow is dead ahead and the smokestack is aft. The temperature—"

"Dry up, will ya?"

"The temperature is mighty hot around the second mate. What's eatin' you, Harry?"

"I'll tell you," he said suddenly very softly, so Johnny couldn't hear. "It was my bunk. It was full of spikes. I could feel 'em, but I couldn't see 'em. I've got the blue willies, third." He mopped his expansive face.

I slapped him on the back and went aft laughing. I was sorry I had laughed. When I turned in to my bunk it was full of cold, wet worms that crept and crawled and sent me mooning and shuddering to the deck, to roll up in the carpet for some shut-eye. No, I couldn't see them.

We left there—wherever "there" was—about fourteen hours after we struck. What it was that had stopped the ship we never did find out. We took soundings all around and got nothing but deep water. Whatever it was that the ship was lying on was directly underneath the turn of the bilge, so that no sounding lead could strike it. After the first surprise of it we almost got used to it—it and the fog, thick as banked snow, that covered everything. And all the while the "loading" went on. When it began, that invisible crowding centered around the section of the starboard well deck that was awash. But in a few hours it spread to every part of the ship. Everywhere you went you saw nothing and you actually felt nothing; and yet there was an increasing sense of being crowded—jostled.

It happened at breakfast, 7:20. The skipper was there, and the mate, though he should have been on the bridge. Harry rolled in, too, three hundred pounds of fretful wanness. I gathered that there were still spikes in his bunk. Being second mate, his watch was the twelve to four, and breakfast was generally something he did without.

The captain lolled back in his chair, leaning against the canted deck and grinning. It made me sore. I refused the bottle he shoved at me and ordered my eggs from the messman.

"Na, don't be dat vay," said the skipper. "Everyt'ing is under control. Ve is all going to get a bonus, and nobody is going to get hurt."

"I don't savvy you, cap'n," I said brusquely. "Here we are high and dry in the middle of an African peasouper, with everything aboard gone haywire, and you're tickled to death. If you know what's going on, you ought to tip us off."

The mate said, "He's got something there, captain. I want to put a boat over the side, at least, and have a look at what it is that's grounded us. I told you that last night, and you wouldn't let a boat leave the chocks. What's the idea—don't you want to know?"

The captain dipped a piece of sea bread into the remains of four eggs on his plate. "Look, boyss, didn't I pull y'u out of a lot of spots before dis? Did I ever let y'u down yet? Heh. Vell, I von't now."

The mate looked exasperated. "O.K., O.K., but this calls for a little more than seamanship, skipper."

"Not from y'u it don't," flared the captain. "I know vat goes on, but if I told y'u, y'u wouldn't believe it. Y'u'll make out all right."

I decided to take matters into my own hands. "Toole, he's got some silly idea that the ship is out of our hands. Told me the other night. He's seeing ghosts. He says we were surrounded by 'vimmin mit tails on.' "

The mate cocked an eyebrow at the Old Man. The captain lurched to his feet.

"Vell, it's true! An' I bat y'u y'ur trip's pay against mine dat I gat one for myself! Ve is taking on a cargo of—" He swallowed noisily and put his face so close to mine that our foreheads nearly touched. "Vare de hell y'u t'ink I got dis viskey?" he bellowed. "Somebody has chartered dis ship, and ve'll get paid. Vot y'u care who it is? Y'u never worried before!" He stamped out.

Harry laughed hollowly, his four pale chins bobbing. "I guess that tells you off, third."

"I'll be damned," I said hotly. "I trust the Old Man as much as anyone, but I'm not going to take much more of this."

"Take it easy, man," soothed Harry. He reached for the canned milk. "A lot of this is fog and imagination. Until the skipper does something endangering crew, ship or cargo we've got no kick."

"What do you call staying in his room when the ship rams something?"

"He seems to know it's all right. Let it go, mate. We're O.K., so far. When the fog clears, everything will be jake. You're letting your imagination run away with you." He stared at Toole and upended the milk can over his cup.

Ink came out.

I clutched the edge of the slanting table and looked away and back again. It was true enough—black ink out of a milk can I'd seen the messman open three minutes before. I didn't say anything because I couldn't. Neither Toole nor Harry noticed it. Harry put the can on the table and it slid down toward Toole.

"All right," said Toole, "we'll keep our traps shut until the skipper pulls something really phony. But I happen to know we have a cargo consigned to a Mediterranean port; and when and if we get off this sandbank, or whatever it is, I'm going to see to it that it's delivered. A charter is a charter." He picked up the can and poured.

Blood came out.

It drove me absolutely screwball. He wouldn't watch what he was doing! Harry was working on a pile of scrambled eggs, and the mate was looking at me, and my stomach was missing beats. I muttered something and went up to the bridge. Every time there was some rational explanation developing, something like that had to happen. Know why I couldn't pipe up about what I had seen? Because after the ink and the blood hit their coffee it was cream! You don't go telling people that you're bats!

It was ten minutes to eight, but as usual, Johnny Weiss was early. He was a darn good quartermaster— one of the best I ever sailed with. A very steady guy, but I didn't go for the blind trust he expressed in the skipper. That was all right to a certain extent, but now—

"Anything you want done?" he asked me.

"No, Johnny, stand by. Johnny—what would you do if the officers decided the captain was nuts and put him in irons?"

"I'd borry one of the Old Man's guns an' shoot the irons off him," said my quartermaster loconically. "An' then I'd stand over him an' take his orders."

Johnny was a keynote in the crew. We were asking for real trouble if we tried anything. Ah, it was no use. All we could do was to wait for developments.

At eight bells on the button we floated again, and the lurch of it threw every man jack off his feet. With a splash and a muffled scraping, the *Dawnlight* settled deeply from under our feet, righted herself, rolled far over to the other side, and then gradually steadied. After I got up off my back I rang a "Stand-by" on the engine-room telegraph, whistled down the skipper's speaking tube, and motioned Johnny behind the wheel. He got up on the wheel mat as if we were leaving the dock in a seaport. Not a quiver! Old Johnny was one in a million.

I answered the engine room. "All steamed up and ready to go down here!" said the third engineer's voice. "And I think we'll have that generator running in another twenty minutes!"

"Good stuff!" I said, and whistled for the skipper. He must have felt that mighty lurch. I couldn't imagine why he wasn't on the bridge.

He answered sleepily: "Vell?"

"We're afloat" I spluttered.

"So?"

"What you want to do—lay here? Or are we going some place?"

There was silence for a long time—so long that I called and asked him if he was still on the other end of the tube.

"I vas getting my orders," he said. "Yes, ve go. Full speed ahead."

"What course?"

"How should I know? I'm through now, third. You'll get y'ur orders."

"From Toole?"

"No!"

"Hey, if you ain't captain, who is?"

"I vouldn't know about dat. Full speed ahead!" The plug on his end of the tube clicked into place, and I turned toward Johnny, uncertain what to do.

"He said full ahead, didn't he?" asked Johnny quietly.

"Yeah but—"

"Aye, aye, sir," he said with just a trace of sarcasm, and pulled the handle of the telegraph over from "Stand-by" to "Full ahead."

I put out my hand, and then shrugged and stuck it

in my pocket. I'd tell Toole about it when I came off watch. "As you go," I said, not looking at the compass.

"As she goes, sir," said Johnny, and began to steer as the shudder of the engines pounded through the ship.

The mate came up with Harry at noon, and we had a little confab. Toole was rubbing his hands and visibly expanding under the warmth of the bright sun, which had shone since three bells with a fierce brilliance, as if it wanted to make up for our three days of fog. "How's she go?" he asked me.

"Due west," I said meaningly.

"What? And we have a cargo for the Mediterranean?"

"I only work here," I said. "Skipper's orders."

Harry shrugged. "Then west it is, that's all I say," he grunted.

"Do you want to get paid this trip?" snapped Toole. He picked up the slip on which I had written the ship's position, which I'd worked out as soon as I could after the sun came out. "We're due south of the Madeiras and heading home," he went on. "How do you think those arms shippers are going to like our returning with their cargo? This is the payoff."

Harry tried to catch his arm, but he twisted away and strode into the wheelhouse. The twelve-to-four quartermaster hadn't relieved Johnny Weiss yet.

"Change course," barked the mate, his small, chunky body trembling. "East-nor'east!"

Johnny looked him over coolly and spat. "Cap'n changes course, mate."

"Then change course!" Toole roared. "The squarehead's nuts. From now on I'm running this ship!"

"I ain't been told of it," said Johnny quietly, and steadied on his westerly course.

"Well, by God, I'm the mate!" Toole said. "You've had no orders from that lunatic to disregard a command of a superior officer. Steer east!"

Weiss gazed out of the wheelhouse window, taking his time about thinking it over. The mate had made his point; to refuse further would be rank insubordination. Though Johnny was strong in his loyalty to the skipper, he was too much of a seaman to be pig-headed about this until he knew a little better where he stood.

"East it is, sir," he said, and his eyes were baleful. He hauled at the wheel, and a hint of a grin cracked his leathery face. "She—won't answer, sir!"

I saw red. "Go below!" I growled, and butted him from behind the wheel with my shoulder. He laughed aloud and went out.

I grasped the two top spokes, hunched my shoulders and gave a mighty heave. There was suddenly no resistance at all on the wheel, and my own violence threw me heels over crupper into the second mate, and we spun and tumbled, all his mass of lard on top of me. It was like lying under an anchor. The wind was knocked out of him, and he couldn't move. I was smothering, and the mate was too surprised to do anything but stare. When Harry finally rolled off me it was a good two minutes before I could move.

"Damn that quartermaster," I gasped when we were on our feet again.

"Wasn't his fault," wheezed Harry. "He really tried to spin the wheel."

Knowing Johnny, I had to agree. He'd never pull anything like that. I scratched my head and turned to the mate. He was steering now, apparently without any trouble at all. "Don't tell me you can turn the ship?"

He grinned. "All it needed was a real helmsman," he ribbed me. And then the engines stopped, and the telegraph rang and spun over to "Stop," and the engine-room tube squealed.

"Now what?"

"I dunno," came the third's plaintive voice. "She just quit on us."

"O.K.; let us know when you've shot the trouble." The engineer rang off.

"Now what the hell?" said the mate.

I shrugged. "This is a jinxed trip," I said. I verified the "Stop" signal on the telegraph.

Harry said: "I don't know what's got into you guys. The skipper said somethin' about a new charter. He don't have to tell us who gave it to us."

"He don't have to keep us in the dark, either," said Toole. Then, glancing at the compass, he said, "Looka that! She's swingin' back to west!"

I looked over his shoulder. Slowly the ship was turning in the gentle swell, back to due west. And just as she came to 270° on the card—the engines began to pound.

"Ah!" said the mate, and verified the "Full ahead" gong that had just rung.

The third whistled up again and reported that he was picking fluff off his oilskins. "I'm going on the wagon," he said. "She quits by herself and starts by herself, an' I'm gonna bust out cryin' if it keeps up!"

And that's how we found out that the ship, with this strange cargo, insisted on having her head. For every time we tried to change course, the engines would stop, or a rudder cable would break, or the steering engine would quit. What could we do? We stood our watches and ran our ship as if nothing were the matter. If we hadn't we'd have gone as mad as we thought we already were.

Harry noticed a strange thing one afternoon. He told me about it when we came off watch.

"Y'know that box o' books in the chart room?" he asked me.

I did. It was an American Merchant Marine Library Association book chest, left aboard from the time the ship was honest. I'd been pretty well all through it. There were a few textbooks on French and Spanish, half a dozen detective novels, a pile of ten-year-old magazines, and a miscellaneous collection of pamphlets and unclassifiable.

"Well, about three o'clock I hear a noise in the chart room," said Harry, "an' I have a look. Well, sir, them books is heaving 'emselves up out of the chest and spilling on th' deck. Most of 'em was just tossed around, but a few was stackin' in a neat heap near the bulkhead. I on'y saw it for a second, and then it stopped, like I'd caught someone at the job, but I couldn't see no one there." He stopped and licked his lips and wheezed. "I looks at that pile o' books, an' they was all to do with North America an' the United States. A coupla history books, an atlas, a guidebook to New York City, a book on th' national parks—all sech. Well, I goes back into the wheelhouse, an' a few minutes later I peeks in again. All them books on America was open in different places in the chart room, an' the pages was turnin' like someone was readin' them, only—there just wasn't nobody there!"

What the *hell* was it that we had aboard, that wanted to know about the United States, that had replaced our captain with a string of coincidence, that had "chartered" the ship? I'd had enough. I firmly swore that if I ever got back to the States, police or no, I'd get off this scow and stay off her. A man can stand just so much.

About three days out the torpedo boat picked us up. She was a raider, small and gray and fast and wicked, and she belonged to a nation that likes to sink arms runners. One of the nations, I mean. I had just come off watch, and was leaning on the taffrail when I saw her boiling along behind us, overtaking.

I ran forward, collaring an ordinary seaman. "Run up some colors," I said. "I don't give a damn what ones. Hurry!"

Pounding up the ladder, I hauled Toole out of the wheelhouse, pointed out the raider and dived for the radio shack, which was some good to us now that the generator was going again.

I sat down at the key and put on a headset. Sure enough, in a second or two I heard: "What ship is that? Where from? Where bound?" repeated in English, French, German and Spanish. I'd have called the skipper, but had given him up as a bad job. Toole came in.

"They want to know who we are," I said excitedly. "Who are we?"

"Wait'll I look at the flag the kid is running up," he

said. He went to the door, and I heard him swear and whistle. "Give a look," he said.

Flying from the masthead was a brilliant green flag on which was a unicorn, rampant. I'd seen it—where was it? Years ago—oh, yes; that was it! In a book of English folk tales; that was supposed to be the standard of Oberon and Titania, King and Queen of ... of the fairies, the Little Folk!

Dazed, I turned to the key and began pounding. I didn't even realize what I was sending. Some imp controlled my hand, and not until it was sent did I realize I had said, *"S.S. Princess of Birmingham, Liverpool, bound for Calais with a load of airplane parts!"*

"Thank you!" said the raider, and put a shell across our bow. Toole had gone back to the bridge, and I sat there sweating and wondering what the hell to do about this. Of all stupid things to say to an enemy raider!

The engine vibration suddenly became labored and the ship slowed perceptibly. Oh, of course, the old wagon would pick a time like this to become temperamental! I beat my skull with my fists and groaned. This was curtains.

The raider was abeam and angling toward us. "Heave to!" she kept buzzing through my phones. Through the porthole beside me I could already see the men moving about on her narrow decks. I turned to my key again and sent the commander of the raider some advice on a highly original way to amuse himself. In answer he brought his four swivel guns to bear on us.

The bridge tube whistled. Toole said, "What the hell did you say to him? He's fixin' to sink us!"

"I don't know," I wailed. "I don't know nothing!"

I ripped off the headset and put my elbows on the port ring across the room, staring out to sea with my back to the swiftly approaching raider. And there in the sunny waves was a conning tower, periscope and all!

Now get this. Here we were, lying helpless, going dead slow with crippled engines between a surface raider and a sub. We were meat for anyone working for any government. Most of us were Americans; if the raider took us it would mean an international incident at a time when no one could afford one. If the sub took us, it was the concentration camp for us. Either might, and probably would, sink us. We were outlaws.

I went up on the bridge. No sense doing anything now. If we got into boats, we'd likely be cut down by machine-gun bullets. Toole was frantically tugging at the handle of the engine-room telegraph.

"I'm trying to stop her!" he gasped. "She's going dead slow; there's something wrong with the engines. They're making such a racket back there that the first assistant can't hear the tube whistle. The telegraph is jammed! The helm won't answer! Oh, my God!"

"Where's your quartermaster?"

Toole jerked a thumb toward the bridge ladder. "I sent him aft to run down to the engine room, and he tripped and fell down to the boat deck! Knocked himself out!"

I ran to the port wing and looked out at the sub. True to her kind, she was attacking without asking questions. There was a jet of spume, and the swift wake of a torpedo cut toward us. At the rate we were going, it would strike us just between the after dry-cargo hold—where the "farm machinery" was stowed—and the fire room. It would get both the explosives and the boiler—good night nurse!

And then our "coincidental commander" took a hand. The crippled, laboring engines suddenly raced, shuddered and took hold. Grumbling in every plate, the *Dawnlight* sat down on her counter, raised her blunt nose eight feet, and scuttled forward at a speed that her builders would have denied. In fifty seconds she was doing fourteen knots. The torpedo swept close under our stern, and the raging wash of the tanker deflected it, so that it hurtled—straight toward the raider!

It struck just aft the stem piece, blowing away the gunboat's bow and turning her on her beam ends. She righted slowly, lying far down by the head, and lay helpless. The sub, seeing her for the first time, came to the surface and men tumbled out of the hatches to man her four-incher. She began blasting away at the torpedo boat as fast as she could load, and the raider answered her, two shots to the sub's one. And there we left them, and for all I know they are blasting away yet, far too busy to pay attention to a crummy old tankship. And Toole and I—well, we cried on each other's shoulders for twenty minutes, and then we laughed ourselves sick.

The next four days were straight sailing, but for the pranks that were played on us. The skipper stuck to his cabin; we found out why later, and I can't really blame him. There was still no sign of the mob of beings that could be felt aboard, but for—again—the pranks that were played on us. We stood our watches and we ate our meals and we painted and chipped and scraped as usual. But for the—but I said that before.

Like the time the buff-colored paint the day gang was laying on the after bulkhead turned the steel transparent for forty-eight hours. Behind the bulkhead was the crew's washroom. The view from up forward was exquisite. As the four-to-eight fireman expressed it: "I wouldn't give a damn if the washroom was just fer washin'."

And lots of little things, like a spoonful of salt turning to thumbtacks in the Cajun's best gumbo soup, and live lobsters in the linen locker, and toadstools in the bos'n's stores, and beautiful green grass, an acre of it, with four concentric fairy rings, growing on a flaked hawser in the forward cargo hold; and then there were the dice that, in the middle of a crap game, developed wickedly humorous caricatures of the six ship's officers—including me. That might not seem like much to you; but when you remember how clever they were, and when you could never meet one of your crew without his bursting into fits of laughter when he saw your face—well, it wasn't the best thing in the world for discipline.

About the captain— We got curious, Toole and I, about how he was getting on. He had locked himself in his room, and every once in a while would whistle for more food. He ate fish almost exclusively, in enormous quantities. We decided to do something about it. Some minor pretext to get a peek into his room. He wouldn't come to the door if we knocked; the portholes were the answer. Now, how could we get the curtain off from the outside without the irascible old man's coming out with a gun in each hand? We finally hit on something ideal. We'd get a broken spar with a snaggy end from somewhere, carry it past his porthole, and "accidentally" stick it in, tearing off the curtain and giving us a good look.

I'm sorry we did. We'd no business looking into the Old Man's private life that way. After all, we decided when we batted the wind about it afterward, the Old Man had a right, if he wanted to, to have a . . . a mermaid in his room! We saw her without being seen, and the skipper must have been in the inner room. She was very lovely, and I got a flash of scales and golden hair, and felt like a heel for looking.

Toole and I talked it over one afternoon as we neared the coast. The two of us had seen more of the whole screwy business than anyone else, and besides, Toole was an Irishman. No one will ever know if he was right or not, but his explanation is the only one that will fit all the facts. Pieced together from a two-hour conversation, this is about what he said, and now—I believe him:

"Third, this is a silly trip, hey? Ah, well. There are many things that you or I can't understand, and we're used to them, like the northern lights and the ways of a woman. I think that the skipper sold us out. No; no harm to us." He dragged on his cigar and stared out to sea as he talked. "Something, or somebody, made a deal with him the day after we sailed. Listen; hear that?"

Far out on the beam sounded the steady *smack-splash* of huge schools of porpoise. Oh, yes; they *might* have been porpoise.

"You told me what the skipper said to you about those critters. And they don't act like porpoises. I don't know if it was one of them or not; maybe it was something we couldn't see that talked. I think the skipper could. He's a squarehead, and they're seagoing people, and they know the sea from 'way back. He's been to sea half again as long as the oldest sailor aboard; you know that. I don't have to tell you that the sea is something that we'll never really understand. You can't know *all* about anything, even an atom; and the sea is so *damn* big.

"Well, he was made an offer; and it was probably a lifetime supply of whiskey and a week or so with that m-mermaid we—thought we saw in his room. What was the deal?

"That he should turn over his ship, and the crew to work it, to whatever party it was that wanted it for a trip from the African coast to America. There must have been provisions, if I know the skipper; he's a downy bird. He must have provided that the ship was to be protected against weather and bullets, mines and torps. He must have stipulated that no one aboard was to be harmed permanently, and—I'm sure of this—that ship and cargo were to be returned to him at the end of the trip. Everything else I've guessed at has turned out, hasn't it? Why not that? The only thing that really bothers me is the loss of time, because time is really big money in this racket. But you can bet that the squarehead wasn't beaten down. We'll find out—I'm certain of it.

"Now, about the passengers. Laugh at me and I'll dry up like a clam; but I believe I have the answer. The old country has inhabitants that men have dreamed and sung and written and told about a great deal, and seen more than seldom. I've spent a lot of time off watch reading about 'em, and my mother used to tell me—bless her! Anyway, there was ghosts and pixies, goblins and brownies, and dervishes and fairies and nymphs and peris and dryads and naiads and kelpies and sprites; gnomes and imps and elves and dwarves and nixies and ghouls and pigwidgeons, and the legion of the leprechauns, and many another. And some were good and some were not, and some helped and some hindered; but all were mischievous as hell. They weren't too bad, any more than are the snakes and spiders that eat mosquitoes, and many were downright beneficial.

"There's hell to pay in Europe now, third. You can't expect a self-respectin' pixie to hide in a shell hole and watch a baby torn to shreds. They sickened of it, and their boss man, whoever he is, got 'em together and and made arrangements to ship 'em someplace where there's a little peace and quiet once in a while, where they can work their harmless spells on a non-aggressive populace. They can't swim worth a damn, and you couldn't expect the sea folk to ferry 'em over; they're an unreliable lot anyway, to all accounts.

"I read a book once about Ol' Puck, and how the Little People were brought to the British Isles from the Continent. They couldn't swim even that, and they got a blind man to row and a deaf mute to stand lookout, and never a word was said of it until Puck himself told of it. This is the twentieth century, and it's a big ocean they've got to cross, and there are many more of them. Did ye notice, by the way," he broke off suddenly, "that though our tanks are empty an' we've used fuel and water and stores for near two weeks, that we're *low in the water?*" He laughed. "We've many and many of 'em aboard.

"We'll unload 'em, and we'll get our pay for the job. But this I'll tell you, and now you may laugh, for you're in the same boat. We're r'arin', tearin' lawbreakers aboard here, third, and we don't give a damn, or we wouldn't be here. But if there's any kind of a good place for us to go at the end of the voyage, then we'll go there for this week's work. It was always a good thing to help a war refugee."

I didn't laugh. I went away by myself and chewed and swallowed that, and I thought about it a bit, and now I believe what I believe, and maybe a little bit more. It's a big world, and these are crazy times.

Well, almost as we expected, we unloaded, but it only took us three hours instead of fourteen. Yes, we struck fog off the Carolinas, and the ship nosed up and heeled over in it, and we could feel the pressure getting less aboard. And when the *thing* under the ship sank and floated us again, and the sun came out—

Well, this is the part that is hard to explain. I won't try it. But look: It was the twenty-third day of September when we sailed from the drydock. And when we lay off the coast that way, just out of the fog, it was the twenty-fifth. And it would have taken just three days for us to reach there from the drydock. Somewhere we lost a week. Yeah.

And the bunkers were full of fuel. And the lockers were full of stores. And the fresh-water tanks were full of water, just as they had been. But—there's a difference. Any fuel we use is—or acts like—high-grade stuff. And our food tastes better, and the work is easier. Yeah, we're lawbreakers—outlaws. But we take our ship where we please, when we please, and never a warship do we see, and never a shell or mine touches us. Oh, yeah; they say she's haunted. No; there's another word for it. She is—*enchanted*. We're paid, and we're being paid. And we'll go anywhere and do anything, because we have the best skipper a man ever sailed under, and because, more than any other men on earth, we need not be afraid of death.

But I can't forget that there'll be hell an' all to pay ashore!